DRAWN TOGETHER

Cheryl Maitland works as a commercial artist in London, and is a fan of Kent Gordon, a cartoonist whose daily newspaper strip is published in seventeen countries. Kent is rich and famous — so why does he seek Cheryl out with a work proposition? Even stranger, he then claims she's his fiancée! What is he up to? Working exclusively for Kent at his island hideaway, away from her home and friends, Cheryl wonders what she's let herself in for, especially as she feels a growing attraction to her enigmatic employer . . .

EMMA SAXON

DRAWN TOGETHER

Complete and Unabridged

LINFORD
Leicester

First published in Great Britain in 2014

First Linford Edition
published 2016

A catalogue record for this book is available
from the British Library.

ISBN 978–1–4448–2949–5

Published by
F. A. Thorpe (Publishing)
Anstey, Leicestershire

Set by Words & Graphics Ltd.
Anstey, Leicestershire
Printed and bound in Great Britain by
T. J. International Ltd., Padstow, Cornwall

This book is printed on acid-free paper

1

The Watcher

'Cheryl, will you please come away from that window and finish in the bathroom? We've got less than ten minutes before Mike's here.'

Sue's request brought a sigh of exasperation from her flatmate. But Cheryl loosened her grip on the bath towel that swathed her trim body and strode back across the living room, long legs flashing through a swirl of pastel-blue terry 'Sorry, Sue. He's still there, though, isn't he? And it's irritating me.'

Sue's dark brows lowered in a frown. 'You're right . . . It really does look as though he's watching the flat.'

Cheryl's voice floated from the bathroom, clinging hints of a Northumbrian accent enhanced by her anxiety and the echoing acoustics of the narrow, high-ceilinged room. 'It's the second night running — and tonight we're going out. What on earth do you think he's after? Is he planning to break in?'

Sue realised Cheryl was more than just irritated. She tried to make light of her friend's fears. 'That'd be a joke. He'd have to be crazy to pick our flat — there's nothing worth taking!'

Though very far from being a dull girl, Cheryl didn't respond to Sue's jollying. 'But imagine it. A stranger poking through your personal property. It would be like being seen without your clothes on.'

'Which is how you'll have to go to the party if we're going to leave on time!' Sue reminded her.

'No I won't. Here, zip me up, please!' She swept back into the living room, clutching the shoulder straps of a colourful green silk dress. It was her meagre wardrobe's greatest extravagance, bought off a street-market rack but up to date in cut and colour.

Sue looked relieved. 'Oh, fast work! You look perfectly gorgeous. Perhaps I didn't need to chivvy you along after all.'

'I wouldn't say that.'

Cheryl grinned impishly. 'You know, I'm going to miss your bullying when we leave here. You're so much more practical than me.'

Cheryl and Sue were facing a big upheaval. Redevelopment meant they would shortly have to move out of their north-London flat over a small shop that sold newspapers, magazines, cigarettes, and confectionery. Sue, who was soon to marry Mike Perkins, planned to go back home and live with her parents for the interim. But Cheryl's plans were typically less clear-cut. She had recently split with a boyfriend of four months' standing and had no intention of returning to her northern home town. She had a pressing need inside her to express her own individuality.

What Cheryl really wanted to do was draw cartoons, but she had enough sense to realise she wouldn't be able to support herself with freelance work unless she could sell it on a regular basis, perhaps to one of the few remaining publishers of children's comics. To that end she'd recently submitted samples of her comic drawings to an agency that represented artists in this specialised market. Every day when she collected her mail from the shop downstairs she eagerly shuffled through the bills and circulars, hoping to receive an encouraging answer. So far she'd been disappointed. Was she being over-ambitious?

'Come on, Cheryl!' said Sue. 'No time for dreaming. Here's Mike's car drawing up now.'

'What about Nosey Parker? Is he still prowling on the corner?'

Sue grimaced. ''Fraid so. Pity your hero here isn't a guard dog!' She picked up a huge toy lion off the bed with a mock growl. The curly-maned lion served as a case for Cheryl's nightdress,

4

but his roguish original cavorted daily through the panels of a popular newspaper-strip cartoon in seventeen countries.

'Bubbles isn't my hero!' Cheryl corrected her laughingly, and went to take the toy off Sue, who whisked it away.

'Liar!' she teased. 'You let him share your bed, don't you? And you're always drawing his picture.'

'Well, it's good practice . . . '

Sue giggled. 'I won't ask which 'it' you mean — the drawing or the bed-sharing!'

'Sue!' Cheryl retorted with mock indignation. 'You know perfectly well what I meant. If I could draw cartoons even half as well as Bubbles' Kent Gordon, I wouldn't grumble.'

'I'd say you wouldn't. That clever Kent Gordon must have made a fortune,' Sue said, and added stoutly, 'But you're clever, too, you know.'

Cheryl smiled wryly. 'Optimistic rather than clever.'

Sue scoffed dismissively at that and tossed Bubbles back onto Cheryl's bed. 'Off we go then, or Mike'll think we haven't seen him and start tooting.'

They went downstairs to where Mike was waiting by his faithful old Mini. 'Hop in, can you?' he said, holding a door open. 'There's a guy over there giving me odd looks. Maybe he thinks I'm obstructing the traffic. He's got the look of a copper about him.' He gave Cheryl a broad grin and Sue a quick kiss on the cheek as they ducked into the car. His amiability sat on his generous frame as comfortably as his casual red sweater and black dress jeans.

How lucky Sue was, Cheryl thought wistfully. Mike wasn't her type, yet she liked him for his never-failing good humour, kindness, and generosity.

Sue rejected his suggestion about the watcher scathingly, confident he wouldn't take offence. 'They don't have plainclothes policemen watching for parking infringements. We think he's a

6

prowler with designs on our flat.'

Mike's twinkling blue eyes widened. 'You're kidding me!'

'We are not — but let's forget about it for now, shall we?' Cheryl said emphatically.

Mike glanced round at her keenly as he took the car away from the kerb, then gave a quick shrug. 'Well, if you say so, though if you and Sue reckon the guy's up to no good, we ought to do something about it.'

There was no arguing with Mike's logic, Cheryl acknowledged. What she didn't want was to spoil what promised to be a carefree evening with a circle of acquaintances from the office tower where she and Sue worked. 'We'll see if he's still hanging around when we get back,' she compromised. She expected that would be well after midnight. Surely he would be gone by then. Unless he was some kind of crank ... She suppressed a shiver as scary snatches of horror movies and newspaper crime reports flashed through her mind.

Mike shrugged again. 'OK. And if he is, we ring the police.' Despite his easy-going manner, Mike was a stickler for doing the right thing.

From time to time Cheryl couldn't help wonder at her good luck in having a flatmate with such a reasonable person for a fiancé. There must be times, she felt, when she was in the way, yet never did Mike show anything but unforced courtesy towards her. Sue, she knew, could hardly wait to be his wife, and Mike must feel a similar frustration. They were so completely in love.

If Roy Bingley could have shown half Mike's restraint, Cheryl might still have had her own escort for occasions like this. But no, Roy had tried to rush her into the kind of relationship she hadn't been ready for, and she preferred not to remember the night she'd finally escaped his hot clutches. The incident had brought it home to her that she and Roy hadn't really been meant for one another after all. Emotionally they'd been on different wavelengths.

Sometime, somehow, there would be a man who could kindle the spark of the fire she instinctively knew was in her. But it wasn't Roy, who left her blood cold and unstirred. That was the most charitable explanation to offer. From now on she'd be wary; avoid deep and unwise involvements and keep things light with the opposite sex. Until that right man came along, of course!

The excuse for tonight's party was a house-warming. A friend had moved to a modern semi-detached in a once semi-rural village on the Essex border long since all but absorbed by the town of Harlow.

The party proved disappointing. Too many people crowded into a lounge not designed for their number or the output of the audio system. Conversation in the kitchen, where many of the women sought refuge from the noise, was of the clucky sort. Cheryl wasn't interested in debating the merits of breastfeeding, or colour schemes for the redecorating of the baby's bedroom. She was the last person to believe life should be lived vicariously discussing the minutiae of others' comfortable ruts. So she spent most of the evening in the crowded lounge.

She pressed herself tightly into a corner, nursing successive alco-pops to unpalatable warmth, viewing frivolities through a pair of very singular eyes.

The unattached male who tried to latch on to her was an opinionated junior bank officer. His plummy voice soon cracked from competing with the throbbing dance music and he had to abandon his overtures. Thank goodness, Cheryl thought. She felt dissatisfied and a little bored.

'Did you enjoy yourself?' Sue asked later as they took the main road back to the city.

'Oh, it wasn't too bad,' Cheryl replied. She wasn't going to be a wet blanket. With Mike at her side, Sue would have been blind to the evening's shortcomings, Cheryl knew.

Contrary to Cheryl's earlier expectations, they were back outside their flat
by a quarter past twelve. She'd put the
suspected prowler to the back of her
mind, but as they entered the street her
eyes started probing the shadows of
nearby doorways, and her pulse quickened. 'He's not there,' she said in a
voice full of relief.

'Who's not? Oh, you mean the
mystery man,' Sue said as though he
was the furthest thing from her mind,
which perhaps he was. 'Well, we've got
nothing to worry about then, have we?
Here, I'll let you go up.'

Sue got out of the car and tipped her
seat forward to let Cheryl out from the
back. 'Won't be long, but don't wait up
for me, will you? We'll probably go
round to Mike's place for a nightcap.'

Cheryl switched on the lights in the
living room and kitchen. The flat
seemed as deeply silent and empty as
always when she was there by herself.
What she did next was a complete
departure from her normal behaviour.

On impulse, she went into Sue's unlit bedroom and crossed quickly to the window.

She looked out. The brake lights of Mike's car were just coming on as he reached the next turning, where he would go right. But the red glow that caught Cheryl's eye was not from the car. It was a tiny glimmer. The tip of a cigarette.

The Mini swept round the corner, and the smoker stepped out into the pool of light under a street lamp. He'd been standing in the shadows of a barred, disused gateway in the high wall surrounding a church.

It was the same man they'd seen earlier, Cheryl was certain. The same man who'd been watching yesterday, too. He looked thoughtfully after Mike's car. Then he looked up at the flat. Cheryl's heart beat faster and she stepped back from the window quickly, illogically concerned he would see her, though his gaze was directed at the lighted windows.

Peering cautiously from behind the cover of the open curtains, Cheryl saw him toss his cigarette butt into the gutter with an air of finality. Then he strode away briskly. Moments later, she heard a car engine cough to life nearby. It sounded as though it had been standing cold for a time and the choke was in operation. Cheryl waited but the car didn't come past the flat. The sound receded in another direction.

She got ready for bed, glad the watcher had left and feeling very tired. She wondered if she should leave a note for Sue under the Bubbles magnet on the fridge door, where she'd be sure to see it. But she decided it was unnecessary. Sleep would be far away, and she'd lie awake agonising over the meaning of it all until Sue returned.

She was wrong. More tired than she thought, the last thing she remembered hearing was Mike's car drawing up outside. Then she was deeply asleep.

* * *

13

Cheryl woke around eight thirty the next morning. Momentarily, she was startled by the patterns of sunlight on the ceiling. Had her alarm failed?

Then she remembered it was Saturday and she didn't have to go to work. She relaxed and turned on the bedside radio, keeping the volume low so as not to disturb Sue.

After a few minutes she sat up, yawned, pushed back the loose russet hair that fell across her forehead, threw off the covers, and got out of bed. She went into the kitchen and made some coffee, which she drank from her favourite Bubbles mug. By nine she had breakfasted and dressed, and still Sue's door was shut. With no one to bounce them off, her thoughts went back and forth in her head like a tiger in a cage.

Really, she should be getting stuck into something. Sooner or later she would have to start flat-hunting. Or if she wasn't going to do that today, she could be polishing her drawing skills. Instead, she was still fretting over the man who'd been watching the flat.

Perhaps there was some mail to take her mind off it. For the past few weeks she'd been living in hope of receiving an encouraging reply from Robinson's Press Art Services. She was sure the samples she'd sent to the agency had been the best cartoon work she'd ever done. Though it was immodest, she felt Kent Gordon himself could scarcely have bettered some of the black and white work. She'd finally mastered the delicate technique of feathering, and details such as shadows, wrinkles and shine marks were bringing life and dimension to her characters.

She crept out of the flat, leaving the door ajar, and went downstairs to the newsagent's. Shopkeeper Tom Simcock was dealing with a customer's query about their bill for paper deliveries, but he caught Cheryl's eye as she went to the pigeonhole where he put the flat's mail.

'Hi, Cheryl. Hang on half a mo, can

you?' He gave her a friendly wink and turned back to his customer.

Cheryl shuffled through the day's mail — a couple of bills and a postcard from a friend of Sue's holidaying in Majorca, and a typewritten letter addressed to herself. She brought it to the top with slightly trembling fingers. The postmark was London, EC4. This had to be from Robinson's Press Art Services!

She had a mad urge to dash back upstairs to open it immediately but knew that would be rude to Tom. So she stood, turning the good-quality white envelope this way and that, till Tom broke the spell.

'Sorry about that, love, but there's something a bit funny I wanted to ask you about.'

'Funny . . . ?'

'Well, peculiar-like. There was this fella came in here yesterday asking questions about the flat. But I got the idea later on he was pumping me for info about yourself.'

'Oh!'

'Course, I gave 'im a flea in the ear, politely enough though.'

Cheryl forced herself to speak with a calmness she didn't feel. 'I see . . . And did this man say who he was?' She knew it had to be the mysterious prowler.

'No. I thought at first he might be a friend of yours from up north, but it seemed unlikely. He didn't have the right accent, and he behaved more like a debt collector or something.'

Cheryl couldn't begin to wonder what the 'or something' might be, and was annoyed to think that a stranger's prying might threaten to damage Tom's opinion of her. She sighed. 'Tom, I haven't a clue who this man is, or what he's up to, but I think it must be the same person who's been watching the flat for several days. Sue and I are quite worried.'

Tom frowned ferociously and grunted. 'You don't say! Well, we don't have to stand for that. Next time he

17

comes lurking around here, he'll have some questions to answer.' He thumped a big clenched fist on the counter. The gesture reminded Cheryl that he was a former amateur boxer of minor note, even though he was nowadays carrying too much weight in the wrong places.

'Don't get yourself into trouble over us, will you?' she pleaded hurriedly.

Tom laughed at her sudden concern. 'No fears. But now I know where I stand, there'll be straight talking, I promise you.' As another customer came into the shop, he said, 'We'll have a yarn about it later, eh?'

Cheryl went back upstairs, pushing the prowler determinedly to the back of her mind in anticipation of opening the letter.

Sue was putting bread into the toaster. 'Late nights don't really agree with me,' she groaned, rubbing her eyes. 'Don't let me stay out after midnight again, will you?'

Cheryl smiled to herself. 'Sue dear,

you know you don't mean that,' she said brightly.

Sue peered at her questioningly. 'You sound as though you're about to burst into song. What's the excitement?'

'Post!' Cheryl seized a table knife and slit open the expensive envelope. Her eyes lit up as she scanned the few brief lines.

'I'm getting somewhere at last, Sue. Listen to this: 'Our director, Mr Harvey Robinson, would like you to telephone me to make an appointment to see him at your earliest convenience.' It must mean he liked my samples. Probably he's going to offer me work!'

Sue took the letter from Cheryl's nerveless fingers and forced her bleary eyes to focus. 'Great . . . great . . . ' she murmured. 'Don't count your chickens though, will you?' she cautioned. 'They haven't committed themselves to anything beyond seeing you.'

After that, the erratic toaster intervened. It wasn't until the smoke and the smell of burning had gone that they came around to the topic of the prowler and Cheryl's new information from Tom Simcock.

'I can't imagine what Tom thinks he can do,' Cheryl finished doubtfully.

'He'll find a way to help, I know he will,' Sue assured her. 'He's got a real soft spot for you, has Tom.'

Despite her professed confidence in Tom's capabilities, Sue was as astonished as Cheryl when less than an hour later one of Tom's delivery boys came thumping up the stairs to the flat. With flushed cheeks, he told them they were wanted urgently in the backroom behind the shop.

'It's a man,' the boy breathed as they went down. 'Mr Simcock saw him across the street an' got me to tell him he wanted a word. Then he told me to get you.' The unusual errand had filled the boy with an air of expectancy. But Cheryl could only feel apprehensive.

Their entry into the small carton-lined room made it crowded. Tom and the stranger, who were sitting either side of the table that filled a third of the space, stood up. The paper boy bobbed behind the two girls, propelling them forward like an energetic sheepdog.

'All right, lad, you can run along now,' Tom told the boy firmly, and Cheryl saw his face fall and read his mind. He wasn't going to be in at the kill he'd sensed was coming.

The stranger thrust a big hand towards Cheryl. 'Miss Maitland, I believe.' He sounded sure of himself and his gaze was unwavering. He looked older than he had from a distance, and he had the physical stamp of a policeman or ex-policeman. His handshake was solid. 'I'm Arthur Gilbert.'

Cheryl was tongue-tied.

'Mr Simcock here seems to think I owe you and Miss Gooding an apology,' Gilbert continued smoothly. 'Apparently you've noticed me about and got concerned about my intentions.'

Cheryl managed a nod. 'That's right.'

'Nothing sinister, I assure you.' He

flipped a business card on to the table in front of Cheryl. 'I'm a reputable private inquiry agent. Unfortunately, I've slipped a bit in that you've spotted me. I've been commissioned to prepare a confidential report on you — a profile, so to speak.'

Indignant colour rose to Cheryl's face. 'What on earth for?' she demanded.

'That I wouldn't know. Usually these things are linked to credit risk, the screening of an employee, sometimes marital relationships, things like that.'

'I see,' said Cheryl bleakly. 'And may I ask who's paying you for this? Frankly I'm totally baffled. Are you sure you've got the right person?'

Gilbert shook his head. 'Very sure. My clients are a worldwide operation with headquarters in New York. I don't think I've anything to lose by naming them — Amalgamated Features Syndicate Incorporated.'

The thought persisted that she was the victim of mistaken identity, but the name of the company Gilbert gave rang

a bell. It was curiously familiar —
something Cheryl saw every day. Then
she placed it: it appeared in tiny print as
a copyright line on several newspaper
cartoons, usually at right angles to the
normal text. If you weren't interested, it
was the kind of thing that would hardly
be noticed, let alone remembered.

Was a logical explanation coming
after all? There was a silence, and Tom
looked at her enquiringly.

'I don't follow,' she said. 'The name's
one I've seen, but what's it got to do
with me?'

'I don't know,' Gilbert told her
frankly. 'I assumed you'd had some
dealings with their London agent, Mr
Harvey Robinson.'

The information was as startling as it
was enlightening. 'I see . . . or maybe I
begin to,' she mused cautiously. 'Tell
me more.'

Gilbert shrugged. 'There is no more.
You'll have to ask Mr Robinson.'

The detective's coolness was infuriating, but oddly it helped her muster a

matching calm. 'I'll do that,' she said with composure. 'It's unfair to take things out on servants who bring unwelcome messages, isn't it? But if you see Mr Robinson before I do, you can tell him I'll be taking up his invitation to meet him, and I'll expect an explanation for this — this snooping.'

For the time being, Cheryl had to let the matter rest. The offices of Robinson's Press Art Services would be closed for the weekend, but she would ring early on Monday.

'Be in first. Don't let on you know about their detective,' Sue advised. 'Make your appointment, get along there face to face with this Robinson — then let him have it!'

But by Sunday evening, Cheryl's resolve was weakening. Supposing Robinson had some work to offer her? On the other hand, did she want to do business with someone who could behave so sneakily?

The next morning, Harvey Robinson's secretary took her call brightly and efficiently and arranged for Cheryl to see her employer at 12.30 p.m. Tuesday. Cheryl then arranged with her boss to take an extended lunch break and work as late as necessary to compensate. She mumbled about having a personal appointment and hoped he would assume she was going to the doctor's or dentist's.

Cheryl couldn't put the mystery to the back of her mind for more than a few minutes at a time, and by Tuesday she'd had three nights of only fitful sleep. She even began to wonder if she had done something wrong. The Amalgamated Features copyright line appeared on Bubbles strips among others.

'Do you think I followed Kent Gordon's style too closely in my portfolio?' she asked Sue anxiously. 'I'd hate them to be dealing with me as a plagiarist.'

She nervously flicked through a fat file of 'swipes' — the helpful drawings and photographs she used as references for her own art. She was appalled at how many of them were clipped from admired Bubbles cartoons. Why hadn't she realised?

Sue just laughed. 'Imitation is the sincerest form of flattery, isn't it? Besides, you don't actually copy them, and you haven't sold anything yet either.'

The building that housed Robinson's Press Art Services didn't match Cheryl's expectations of a shimmering glass office tower. It was ten minutes' walk from the Underground — she wondered whether she wouldn't have done better to go on to the next station — and it was red Victorian brick that had seen better days. Robinson's offices were on the third floor behind a creaking door with a black-lettered frosted-glass panel.

She gave her name to the receptionist, who buzzed for Robinson's secretary. Cheryl recognised the bright, efficient voice she'd spoken to over the phone, but the woman was older than she'd imagined, and unexpectedly matronly.

Harvey Robinson, too, was a surprise: no sharp, high-powered salesman type, but a little man, meek and nondescript with greying hair and a moustache. He wore an unfashionable suit of indeterminate but dowdy colour, with a cream shirt and brown tie.

He had a limp handshake. 'Miss Maitland? Very pleased you could call, I'm sure.'

It was at this point, just as she was about to launch into a careful speech about the detective, that she became uncomfortably aware of another person in Robinson's office. He — she was sure it was a he — was behind her, and she could feel his watching eyes.

The hairs on the back of her neck prickled with a weird apprehension. She felt compelled to look round, and when she did, she wished she hadn't. Just then it would have been better for her confidence if this man had stayed as that hint of a presence. Once she saw him, he became an unnerving reality.

He was lounging in a low chair set against the same wall as the door from the reception area, and was as impressive as Robinson was unimpressive. He rose to his feet with a languid, powerful grace; tall and lean, with collar-length, sun-bleached hair and misty grey-green eyes in a bronzed face. If he hadn't been wearing an expensive leather jacket, classic blue jeans and an open-necked pink shirt, he could have been a Nordic pirate of long ago. His teeth gleamed between full lips that curved in a bright smile.

Nothing about him could be called dull. Cheryl was dazzled. 'Hello there,' he said as her eyes met his. His voice was resonant with a confident masculinity and a slight accent strange to her. Nor could she put an age to him, except he was some years older than herself and the men she usually mixed with socially.

In looks he was a knockout. He had all the presence of a screen idol and more. But Cheryl was watching no movie. This was real life. She couldn't sit back and watch and be thrilled. She had to speak — yet she was ridiculously dry-mouthed and tongue-tied.

'Oh yes . . . ' Robinson's reedy voice came to the rescue, ending the first uncomfortable moment. 'Let me introduce one of our group's most successful artists. He's quite a celebrity, in fact — '

'Harvey! Cut it out, will you?' The younger man sounded more amused than impatient. 'Look, you're embarrassing Miss Maitland. Perhaps you should call me in later?'

Robinson cleared his throat and blinked. 'Yes, well . . . I mean, no — you must stay,' he insisted. Then, in a rush, he added, 'Miss Maitland — Kent Gordon, creator of the world-famous Bubbles strip.'

Cheryl gulped. Her heart pounded. Kent Gordon! What was going on here? She'd dreamed that one day she might meet this giant among cartoonists. But it had been the idle dream of a fan who knows at heart the object of her admiration must stay forever distant. Kent Gordon was a millionaire, wasn't he? In recent years he'd lived in near-seclusion on his own private island off the coast of New Zealand — a whole world away.

Realising how gormless she must appear, seemingly struck with paralysis and bereft of speech, Cheryl made a supreme effort to put the remarkable development aside and steer her encounter with Harvey Robinson back on to the course she and Sue had discussed.

'I'm delighted to meet you, Mr Gordon.' She gave him a nod. How inadequate it sounded! She was overwhelmed. 'But before we go any further, Mr Robinson, I have to tell you I'm not very happy with what's been going on since I wrote to you.'

Robinson ran a finger round the collar of his shirt as if it had become too tight. 'Hmm ... now what exactly are you referring to?' He looked flustered.

'You know!' Cheryl blurted. She was acutely conscious of Kent Gordon's raised eyebrows but determined to ignore him. 'This private detective you've had spying on me! It's an invasion of privacy, and I want to know what you mean by it!'

Robinson looked extremely put out. He pulled a handkerchief from his pocket and dabbed his brow. 'I can understand . . . yes, of course,' he dithered.

Kent Gordon stepped up alongside the unfortunate man with a friendly smile, seeming to take in every inch of her. It was as though the impact of his attention was physical. He could have struck her and she wouldn't have been more shocked, more stunned. She stood perfectly still.

'Miss Maitland — Cheryl — I think it would help if I did the explaining.'

Cheryl's heart turned over as he casually slipped in that use of her first name. But what he said next sent it hammering to her throat and brought heat flaring to the surface of her skin.

'You see, it wasn't Harvey's idea to hire the detective. It was mine.'

2

A Fantastic Proposition

For several moments there was only the muffled sounds of voices from the outer office and traffic on nearby Farringdon Road. Just as Cheryl had been starting to regain her equilibrium, this man had thrown her off balance again. She could hardly believe she'd heard correctly. But his apologetic expression told her she had.

'You did?' she said at last, finding herself weakening under the influence of his undeniable charm.

'I'm afraid so.'

Then she felt suddenly resentful that he should have taken the wind out of her sails and made her cheeks burn. She'd been about to tell Robinson exactly what she thought of his underhanded prying and demand to know the reason for it. That Kent Gordon was younger, incredibly handsome, talented, and rich, didn't change a darned thing.

'Why did you do it, Mr Gordon?' She tried to sound contemptuous. But the very idea he should be remotely interested in her was so surprising and embarrassing — yet strangely elating, that it made her voice croaky when she wanted it to be icy.

He had no trouble in putting the question aside. He raised both his hands to chest height, palms outward towards Cheryl, brown fingers spread and pointing upwards. 'The answer isn't a quick one. Please — let's make ourselves comfortable.' His open hands seemed to say he had nothing to hide. Cheryl wanted to believe it.

Robinson hopped behind him like a grey sparrow as he turned to a low table ringed by chairs. 'Not that we can divulge too much at this stage,' the agent put in hastily.

Cheryl caught Kent Gordon's fleeting frown. He'd recognised that what

34

Robinson said would be no help in placating her. That was shrewd. Could she trust such a man? He moved one of the seats out for her.

'Tea or coffee, Cheryl? Harvey's people are very good at either. None of your office instant.'

Robinson took his cue and played host, then Kent began to talk. 'There's nothing sinister to it at all. We've been looking for someone special to take on a very important job.' He shook his head and gave her a wry, disarming smile. 'And believe me, it's been a tedious process — hasn't it, Harvey?'

'Oh yes . . . months have gone into it, not just here but in the States, across the continent, Scandinavia . . . '

'I thought we'd found what we wanted six weeks ago — a guy in Copenhagen who'd done some marvellous stuff for the Disney comic books produced there. That is, until a drink problem got the better of him.'

Robinson tutted. 'Quite unsuitable. Unreliable type . . . lived with three different women in four years and had children by all of them.'

'All sorts of complicated ties and distractions, you see,' Kent went on. 'So this time, we did our homework. Your portfolio was extremely promising. It demonstrated most of the artistic attributes we were seeking.'

Cheryl didn't know what to say. She twisted her hands together. 'So you were looking for an artist,' she said tentatively.

Kent put his coffee cup down on the table and leaned forward. 'More than that. A person we can depend upon and who's available and willing to devote him- or herself to a particular assignment in a very total way.'

His earnestness was slightly frightening. 'It sounds . . . demanding. I'm flattered that you like my drawings, of course. Presumably you intend to offer me this job?'

Kent and Robinson exchanged glances and Robinson nodded. 'Yes, we do,' Kent said. 'But first I should tell you it involves a two-year-minimum contract with a clause stipulating the employee is prepared to work in any place in the world as directed by Amalgamated Features Syndicate.'

'And that the nature of the work done shall be kept strictly confidential,' added Robinson swiftly.

They both studied her with an intent air of expectation. Because she was at a loss for words, Cheryl found their gaze doubly discomfiting.

'It really is quite unlike anything I had in mind,' she got out nervously, her eyes dropping to her clenched hands. 'I don't know . . . this travel . . . I don't understand.'

She sensed that her lack of enthusiasm worried Kent. Irrationally, she thought. She hadn't rejected the proposition point-blank. And she could have; it sounded outlandish enough.

'The money is exceptionally good,' he said, an anxious edge to his voice. 'You would be paid in US dollars, and it would be the equivalent of fifty thousand pounds for each of the two years.'

For Cheryl, the amount was breath-taking. 'That's fantastic!' she gasped involuntarily. 'I mean, it's more than twice my present salary. Do you really think I could earn it?'

Her ingenuous amazement restored a smile to Kent's lips, and that tripped a quickening in her heartbeat she didn't want to recognise.

'Of course. It's what the job's worth. Whoever does it will deserve every cent, and I think you could do it.'

A plague of doubts assailed her. What were these two playing at? The unbelievable hundred thousand pounds was tempting — but frightening, too. What would be expected of her for this kind of money? And Robinson's demand for secrecy made her uneasy.

Cheryl sighed and shook her head. 'I'll admit I'm interested, but I don't want to make a fool of myself, and it sounds . . . well, risky.'

Kent raised an eyebrow. 'Risky?

Don't tell me you've lost the spirit of adventure that brought you to London! Surely something worthwhile and rewarding calls for taking chances?' He looked her straight in the eyes as though he sought to probe behind them. 'Don't disappoint me, Cheryl. It must sound a bit of a gamble, I know, but what's at stake? Your friend Sue is about to get married, and the lease on your flat is almost up and can't be renewed. You've already cut your ties with your childhood home, so I can't see you running home to Mum and Dad.'

She bit her lip, almost scared to reply. His boldness was challenging, his level gaze daring her. 'That detective has been earning his money, hasn't he?' she stalled. She couldn't deny a word he'd said, and she didn't want to refuse him, but the snooping that backed his insight annoyed her. 'No, I don't intend to rush back to my mother and stepfather.' She laid careful emphasis on the correction.

He raised an eyebrow interrogatively — a further wordless expression of his effrontery that snapped her control. 'It really was no business of yours,' she said with sweet sarcasm, 'but as I'm sure you've so cleverly found out, relations are strained. Among other things, they reckon I'm wasting my talents after dropping out of an art course at a technical college in Newcastle.'

'And you don't see it their way.'

'Of course not! London is a far better base for a commercial artist.'

'Ah! So you're quite content with your present position?' His voice was tinged with regret.

'I didn't say that. But being a junior assistant to the art director of an advertising agency does at least have the sound of a real job description.'

Now she had got going, the words were tumbling out of her mouth, clipped and critical. Her own courage amazed her. 'Frankly, any intelligent person would question what you're offering. It's incredible!'

'The arrangements proposed must seem puzzling to you; bizarre, even,' Kent admitted. 'It would help if we could say more, I realise ... ' He glanced aside at Robinson, who said nothing, but frowned and shook his head. 'Once the contract has been signed and so on, I'm sure my business people will agree to reveal a lot more,' Kent pressed on persuasively. 'But the next step is yours.'

He leaned closer to her, flatteringly attentive, waiting for her answer. A silence fell. He stretched out a hand and lightly squeezed her arm. 'You won't regret it,' he prompted quietly.

His unexpected touch drove a surge of adrenaline through her veins. It was difficult to keep a clear head. 'All right ... I'll think about it,' Cheryl compromised haltingly.

Kent was relieved. She saw the tension ebb from his body, and his posture became relaxed. Faint lines in his face — of strain? — were softened by his broad smile. 'That's great! My biggest fear was that you'd turn us down flat and we'd be back to square one.'

'I'm not committing myself,' Cheryl reminded him quickly.

'Of course not. But you'll think the proposition over and you'll realise it's too good to let go by.'

'You sound confident.'

'I am. See me again tomorrow. Have dinner with me at my hotel.'

Cheryl knew she was hooked. *I'm powerless, like a fish on a line*, she thought as he named a very grand establishment in Mayfair.

'Hopefully you'll be able to let me know your decision then, and we can start making arrangements.'

It was just the escape Cheryl needed. She didn't have to say yes and she didn't have to say no. Not yet. 'Thank you,' she said simply, feeling relief that the pressure was off for the moment. 'I'd like that.'

Robinson was pleased, too. 'A first-rate idea,' he enthused, rubbing his hands together. He'd been itching for an excuse to end this awkward interview ever since Cheryl had stormed at him about the sneaky private detective. Now it was over, so if she later rejected the proposal, it wouldn't be in his offices and the responsibility wouldn't fall so heavily on his narrow shoulders.

Everybody seemed to mill around in the reception area while Robinson's matronly secretary put her efficient telephone manner to work, organising a taxi to take Cheryl to Kent's hotel for the dinner appointment next evening.

'And let's have another taxi to take Cheryl back to work now,' said Kent thoughtfully when the secretary had finished. He was smiling at her again — that cool, charming smile that had already turned her knees to water.

Cheryl shied at the suggestion. 'Oh, no,' she said. 'I'd much rather go by tube. It's almost as quick; perhaps quicker than waiting.'

She didn't like the idea of hanging around here, or of turning up outside the advertising agency's windows in a taxi. If she were spotted, the extravagance might spark conjecture and questions. She could do without a tussle with the office rumour machine.

★　★　★

The Circle Line's alternate plunges into artificial light and daylight heightened the mood of unreality that had settled over her. A dream couldn't be more amazing than the last hour. But she didn't have to pinch herself to know she was awake. She really had met Kent Gordon, and she was dining with him tomorrow night! What was more, he was offering her a job!

Concentrating on her work that afternoon was an effort. The day seemed endless. She had to rescale some used artwork so it could be incorporated in a new series of advertisements of different column widths. Her tussle with the computer went to three rounds before she'd satisfactorily incorporated the reduced images into the fresh layouts. 'I don't know what's wrong with me,' she fibbed to her boss.

Meanwhile, she told herself she was being all kinds of an idiot. It was ridiculous even to think of throwing in a secure, if mundane, job to go chasing after something so dubious. The hundred thousand pounds were riches indeed, but . . . There were so many buts. She argued back and forth with herself ceaselessly.

Through it all ran the recurring image of Kent Gordon. Despite her long-time admiration of his work, she had never wondered what he would be like as a person. She'd perhaps imagined he would be some kind of cartoon character himself — a roly-poly, jovial man of middle age. She couldn't remember. That part of her memory had been totally wiped since meeting him. She could still see the bronzed, slightly craggy features, the wavy blond hair, the full-lipped smile, the lithe movements he made. His lean, powerful frame told her he didn't spend the whole of his life hunched over a drawing board. Where was this 'any place in the world'? Would she go there with him?

By five thirty, she was dying to get home to the flat. There she would be able to talk some of these things out with Sue instead of pursuing them in circles inside her head. But the building was nearly empty and it had gone way past six before she felt she could fairly pack away her equipment for the day and head off. She'd taken at least an extra twenty minutes at lunch break, and frankly her performance since had been lacklustre.

Cheryl got to Liverpool Street Station just in time to jump aboard the suburban train that was two later than the one she normally caught. At least she could have a seat, she thought gladly as it drew away with a jerk. She still felt oddly weak-kneed.

The rush to the mainline station had kept her frustration under control, but by the time the train was clattering through Bethnal Green it had all built up again and she was bursting with impatience. She couldn't wait to see the look on Sue's face when she heard the story of the interview.

Sue had a risotto simmering when she arrived at the flat, a little breathlessly. 'I'm home!' she cried. 'I thought I'd never get here.'

Sue swung round from the cooker. 'I hope you're hungry. It's ready when you are . . . ' Then she saw the glow on Cheryl's face. 'Come on then,' she urged expectantly. 'Tell me — how did it go?'

'You won't believe it, Sue,' Cheryl began, then rushed into an account of the extraordinary meeting at Robinson's agency.

Sue watched Cheryl with increasing attention as she spoke, taking in how serious and intense she became. She also observed the look of delight that surged into her eyes when she came to Kent Gordon's invitation to dinner. Joy shimmered beneath their hazel surface.

'So you didn't get to finish your big speech about our invaded privacy?'

'Well . . . no,' Cheryl admitted. 'It sort of got brushed aside, but perhaps I'll have a better chance tomorrow.'

Sue hid a disbelieving smile. 'You mean you'll accept his meal at this swank restaurant, then get mad with the man for the worry he caused us before he showed his hand?'

Cheryl looked thoughtful. 'Perhaps not. After all, it is water under the bridge now, isn't it?'

'And what are you going to say to this peculiar contract he's offering? I suppose that's the most important part now.'

Cheryl closed her eyes and sighed. 'It's difficult. I haven't been able to think about anything else all afternoon, and I still don't know.'

'Consider all that money,' Sue prompted.

'I have, believe me! But it's true what they say — money isn't everything. If it had been just Harvey Robinson there, I would have said no right away. He was so jumpy and secretive about everything. Like he knew he was doing something deceitful.'

'But Kent Gordon was different,' Sue said matter-of-factly.

'Sue! You're mocking me, aren't you?'

Sue gave her a playful punch on the shoulder as she went past her to the cutlery drawer. 'Well, admit it . . . he's made a hit with you, hasn't he? And you've always been the number-one fan of that comic strip he draws.'

Cheryl stood her ground. 'He did have a certain charisma, nothing like I would ever have expected,' she confessed seriously.

Sue laughed lightly. 'I was only kidding. Tell me I'm jealous, go on. Not many people get asked out by highly personable millionaires!'

'I'm going to go and find out what else he has to say for himself anyway,' said Cheryl resolutely. 'There's nothing to lose in that, is there?'

'Of course not — you'll even get a sumptuous free meal into the bargain. It sounds great. In fact, I'm all for it. But look after yourself, won't you?'

'Now you're starting to sound like my parents,' Cheryl accused her.

'Heaven forbid! I'd hate to think what your stepfather would say about this.'

'He'd raise the roof with all the obvious objections. But it would be knee-jerk stuff. Mum would be more worried, really.'

'Perhaps you should go home and see them before you make up your mind what you're going to do,' Sue suggested. 'There's this business of having to give up the flat, too, remember? You might have to turn to them eventually.'

Cheryl's voice rose adamantly. 'Never! I wouldn't leave London. I'd go back to the hostel if I had to.'

'But it was appallingly overcrowded and crawling with cockroaches,' Sue bantered back.

'I'd sleep out in a cardboard box then!' Cheryl retorted.

'That would certainly upset your mother.'

Cheryl pondered. 'Maybe ... but Mum's worry is a funny thing. It doesn't take too much to reassure her, if you know what I mean. She wants to be reassured, I suppose. And it's more convenient if I'm down here out of the way. Oh yes, she'll do her duty and tell me I ought to be 'sensible' and come home, but deep down it's better for both of us if I don't.'

How sad, Sue thought, but she said, 'I wonder if she'd feel the same way about you going abroad, though.'

Cheryl shrugged. 'We'll see what happens tomorrow. If I say yes to Kent's offer, I guess I'll have to go up and see them, to say goodbye.'

Sue detected that whatever Cheryl said, her mind was half made up, even if she didn't know it herself. 'Perhaps it would be a good idea for you to find out some more about Kent Gordon yourself . . . play him at his own game.'

Cheryl quickly pointed out the holes in the suggestion. 'Except I can't afford a private detective, and he's hoping for my decision tomorrow. I got the impression he and his crowd have been trying to fill the job for some time. They must be getting desperate to choose me, surely?'

'Don't be so humble!' Sue said with indignant loyalty. 'You've got a load of talent. I'm not clued up on the technical side of things, but I think your drawings are terrific. Let them know you're worth every penny of what they're offering. You haven't been discovered yet, that's all.'

'You reckon?' Cheryl said dryly. 'And maybe I won't be discovered, unless I can create something as outstanding and original as Bubbles.'

'Who knows? Maybe you will one day.'

'But in the meantime I do humdrum chores at an ad agency.'

'Is that so bad?'

'I suppose not, but it's not so good either. It's not what I really wanted.'

'And you think this mysterious job of Kent Gordon's might be?'

'Possibly . . . I just hope he'll tell me more tomorrow.'

Sue frowned in exasperation. 'I still think we ought to know more about the man,' she repeated. 'He's your shining example, cartoon-wise. A role model. You must know something about him as a person.'

Sitting down, Cheryl put her elbows on the table and cupped her face in her hands. 'Not much,' she admitted after a moment's concentration. 'Just the few bits I've seen in papers and magazines. He's a New Zealander, but he spent a good part of his early working life here. He did freelance work for the juvenile market, like I want to. Then after a few years there was Bubbles, and he was rich and famous and — ' She suddenly

53

broke off, her eyes all at once wide, bright and alert. 'I remember! He was married, but it quickly ended in divorce. And before that he'd gone back from Britain to live on a private island off the New Zealand coast. A rugged, out-of-the-way place . . . ' She stopped again, this time swamped by a nervousness that made her stomach revolt at the savoury smell of the waiting risotto.

Sue put her fear into words. 'You think he'll want you to go to New Zealand?'

Cheryl thrust the thought away with a wobbly laugh. 'No, surely not. It's a retreat, a hideaway, as I recall. It's the place where he does all his own brilliant work. He couldn't want the distraction of an unknown novice there.' But her cheeks had taken on an embarrassed flush.

'Couldn't he?' Sue teased.

Cheryl swallowed hard. 'Oh, come on! A man in his position doesn't have to stoop to such tricks to get himself a — a companion!'

Sue scrutinised her as though she were seeing her for the first time. She decided Cheryl probably had a lot going for her when it came to appealing to the opposite sex. 'I was just joking, really,' she said. 'But you know the ways of the world. You mustn't let your admiration for his work and success blind you. Don't let yourself be trapped in a situation you can't handle.'

Cheryl bent her head. 'I may have been pretty naive when I arrived in London, Sue, but I'm not a child anymore.'

'No, of course not. But New Zealand as a cartoonist's work base doesn't sound a very probable scenario.'

'Truth can be stranger than fiction,' Cheryl said, remembering something and perking up. 'Kent Gordon isn't the first famous cartoonist to work from New Zealand. Haven't you heard of Murray Ball? His strips were syndicated worldwide in more than a hundred and twenty publications. You must google him on the net.'

Sue seemed reassured by Cheryl's response to her warnings; Cheryl, though, was not as confident as she'd tried to sound. The unwelcome investigations by Kent Gordon's private detective still cast a shadow over what could have been a glamorous offer to someone with her ambitions. Nor could she overlook the fact that the artist and Robinson had told her very little of substance, except they were prepared to pay big money. What could justify such secrecy?

★   ★   ★

That night she lay awake in bed a long time, staring into the dark and trying to sort things out; trying to guess how it would all evolve.

Finally she drifted into exhausted sleep and a tortuous dream. Kent Gordon and Harvey Robinson were urging her to sign papers. She couldn't make them understand that they were useless, because they'd been drawn up to the wrong size and she couldn't calculate the proper proportions. Kent was unable to help — he had glove puppets on both his hands. One was Bubbles, the other a red-haired child she recognised as a caricature of herself based on an old embarrassing school photograph still kept framed on a sideboard at her parents' home.

*　*　*

'So you're sure Miss Maitland fits the bill?' Harvey Robinson fingered his grey moustache nervously and cast his eyes again over the samples of Cheryl's work spread before him.

Kent Gordon stood tall in front of his desk. 'Positive,' he said firmly. 'Where else have you seen stuff like this?' He stabbed a long finger at one of the larger pieces of Bristol board. 'Look at these panels; that bold, sure touch in the composition. It could almost be my own.'

'For a beginner, she's remarkably

good,' conceded Robinson in his thin voice. 'But she is very young — and a woman.' He emphasised the two words with distaste.

'I *had* noticed,' Kent tossed back lightly. 'Very bright and attractive, too.'

Robinson expanded on his objections. 'In the normal run of things it would hardly matter, I suppose. Her work could speak and stand for itself. But what we're setting up is something quite different ... Two years! She might find it very hard not to break the contract, despite the money.'

Kent hunched his shoulders. 'With luck we might not have to go to the full two years. Who knows? Also, from what we've found out, she's very dedicated and ambitious where her drawing's concerned.'

'Possibly,' Robinson admitted. 'But drawing isn't everything.'

'Perhaps she'll find compensations in the work for the things she might have to miss. And I don't really think it matters that she's a woman. Lois copes.

So does Moira McBride.'

'They're used to it,' Robinson pointed out. 'And perhaps their choice was more deliberate — '

'Harvey,' Kent broke in, 'I'll see to it that Miss Maitland's choice is deliberate, too. She's having dinner with me, remember?' His face became set and cold. 'She was flattered and impressed by our offer — '

It was Robinson's turn to interrupt. 'A bit overwhelmed, I'd say. And you'll recall she was upset — annoyed by the inquiries we'd been making.'

Kent gestured dismissively. 'I can put that right. It won't take much to have her eating out of my hand. In fact, one of the problems may end up being keeping silly ideas out of her head.'

'Ah! You agree then — it would have been better if we'd found a man, or even a much older woman.'

'We haven't,' Kent said with sharp exasperation, 'so that's totally irrelevant. Besides, I've no intention of allowing her gender to become a distraction to either of us. I've been down that road before. It's Cheryl Maitland's artistic talents we're interested in. We wouldn't want her work affected by any sentimental fantasies, would we?'

3

Cheryl Gives Her Word

Cheryl spent the next day feeling far from her best. Her restless night had left her tired and heavy-headed. Again she found it hard to concentrate on her work. And the weather didn't help. A sombre, overcast day was followed as darkness fell by a relentless downpour that lashed at the windows of the flat. Taking pains with hair and makeup for her dinner date seemed unavoidably futile. One stormy gust as she went to and from the taxi and she'd end up looking a wreck anyway. It was an evening for curling up with a good book or watching an undemanding video, and she said as much to Sue.

'That's silly, and you know it,' her friend told her bluntly. 'When it comes to drawing cartoons, this guy's the cat's whiskers, right? And he's offering what might be your big chance. If you back out now, you'll spend the rest of your life wondering about what might have been.'

'Yesterday you were saying I had to be careful.'

'I still do. But I'm all for you keeping this date. I always have been.'

When the taxi drew up outside, Cheryl's heart began to beat a shade faster than usual. The journey to Kent Gordon's hotel took a full forty minutes. Cheryl felt very alone. She hadn't felt like this since the first time she'd caught the train from Newcastle to London, full of curious expectation and nervous excitement.

But why was it that when fresh beginnings loomed, one always had those regretful backward glances? This time it was to Sue and their cosy flat. In a flash of illumination she saw her present situation for what it was in her life — just a brief episode that was now drawing to a natural close, whatever she might hear and decide tonight.

Taxis were not Cheryl's normal mode of transport. You caught a taxi in an emergency. Their atmosphere was pervasively alien and ominous to her. She much preferred them from the outside, as part of the passing London scene. By the time the taxi reached the hotel, even the cutting rain beating in under the canopied entrance was welcome after the stale, slightly damp claustrophobia of the cab's interior.

The few people in the hushed foyer didn't include Kent Gordon, and she made a quick visit to the cloakroom before returning repaired to the front desk. She felt little easier knowing her windswept hair was tidy again and her face dry and unsmudged.

The receptionist said Mr Gordon had left a message that he would be in the bar next to the restaurant.

He had taken a stool placed where the view of the doors was unimpeded. They were face to face across the room as soon as she went in. He wore a white dinner jacket and dark trousers with the same casual ease as leather and denim. The gleaming smile on the tanned face was the same, too. Like a Hollywood Viking, she thought again. He held out both his hands to her as they met halfway across the room.

'I was afraid for a moment you might not come,' he said. 'Now you're here, I'm doubly glad. You look wonderful.'

The brief, welcoming grip of his hands as they caught hers was solid and reassuring. And the compliment was unforced, but not paid so smoothly that she should doubt his sincerity. She felt good, and made up her mind to enjoy the evening.

'Thank you. It was very kind of you to ask me here.'

Sue would have approved of her dignity and composure, Cheryl thought. It didn't betray an iota of her underlying mood of curious expectation and nervous excitement.

'The pleasure is mine, Cheryl.' He spoke genuinely, and the intonation of her name in his unfamiliar, slightly colonial accent gave her a charge of illogical exhilaration.

When he asked if she would like a drink before they ate, she declined. She could feel more at ease with a dinner-table situation, she reasoned swiftly. There were only four other people in the bar — two couples and the room seemed designed for intimacy. Dinner in the hotel's restaurant would be less of a tête-à-tête.

Cheryl's heart was still thumping as a hostess showed them to their table. The room was adequately lit by two elaborate chandeliers suspended from the ornately plastered ceiling. The tables were spaced to give reasonable access. Yet at one place Kent bumped into a chair to one side of their passage. For a split second Cheryl thought he would stumble into a vacant table and send crystal and cutlery cascading to the floor. But he was saved by the almost cat-like grace of his movements, the sureness of step she'd noticed the day before. He recovered his balance in a single pace like an athlete or dancer, and they continued to their own table.

'Sorry,' he muttered almost curtly to the young woman guiding them. 'Didn't see it, that's all.'

Kent and Cheryl were left to study impressive menus in embossed leather folders, and the momentary hitch was forgotten. He was completely charming and courteous. The hotel's cuisine was dictated by its French chef, he explained. 'It's a very benevolent dictatorship, and you'll have no complaints,' he promised.

On Kent's recommendation they began with *Soupe de Moules*. Cheryl enjoyed it so much, she decided to follow his example and have *Poulet Madagaskar* for a main course.

'You'll like it,' he said. 'They stuff a chicken breast with bananas, crumb it with almonds, and serve it with a green pepper sauce.'

They also ordered a bottle of white wine. Cheryl's experience in this department was limited, and though he passed the wine list to her, she was more than glad to let him make the selection.

'This is one of the hotels I know here where they stock New Zealand wines.' He picked a chardonnay. 'It's like a white burgundy, but even better, I feel. It's won several medals in Europe, I understand.'

After a sip or two, Cheryl couldn't fault his taste. 'Mm . . . it's lovely, and chilled to just the right temperature.'

The meal was a perfect success. By the time Cheryl was enjoying a chocolate-topped dessert — it contained whipped cream laced with hazelnut liqueur — she was feeling relaxed and appreciative.

'You know,' said Kent confidingly, 'I really do feel it was a stupid mistake for me to hire that Arthur Gilbert fellow. I might've known he'd turn out to be a clumsy flatfoot! Why he was so indiscreet, I don't know. It must have been very alarming for you and your friend to have had him lurking about the way he did. You will accept my apologies, won't you?'

Cheryl smiled, recognising that his tactics left her disarmed, yet not resenting it. 'You're forgiven,' she said with a laugh. 'How can you not be after such a delicious meal? But I've not forgotten there are strings attached — that you're expecting an answer to your contract offer.'

'That's right,' Kent said, looking her straight in the eye. 'So tell me, now you've had time to think it over . . . How do you feel about it?'

'I want to know more,' she said gravely. 'If I'm put off at all, it's because you and Mr Robinson seem so intent on being secretive.'

Kent thought for a moment. Then, as though reaching a decision, he lightly slapped the damask tablecloth with an open palm. 'Dammit — you're right. Our approach is all wrong. We have to trust you, Cheryl, and I think we can. Where would you like me to start?'

'I want to know what the job is and where it is I have to go,' she said evenly. ''Any place in the world' is so all-encompassing as to be ridiculous.'

'Agreed,' he admitted. 'The 'where' is New Zealand. To be more precise, a privately owned offshore island of thirty-five hectares — that's about eighty acres. Not very encompassing at all, in fact. The 'what' is working as my art assistant. You would be the first and only person in the position, and everything you produced would be the exclusive property of myself and Amalgamated Features Syndicate.'

The simple answers left Cheryl bursting with so many more questions that she hardly knew where to begin. But before she could gather her thoughts, Kent was leaning forward across the table, his hand closing over hers. 'You realise, of course, that whatever you decide, I expect you to keep this completely confidential,' he said earnestly. She looked up from their hands and his eyes again sought and held hers. 'The syndicate and I don't want it to become public knowledge that someone else might be responsible, even partly, for the Bubbles strips.'

Cheryl frowned. The touch of his hand on hers was distractingly stirring, yet her mind was very clear. 'But surely the top artists frequently have less experienced assistants in their studios. I should have thought nearly everyone takes that for granted.'

'Why, yes, they probably do. There's a difference here, though. You're talking about the routine work — filling in the blacks without being sloppy, tidying up the inks generally, a bit of lettering and so forth. What we want is much more than a novice; someone capable of playing a bigger part.'

'It's still got me puzzled,' Cheryl confessed, shaking her head.

'Let's put it another way then,' Kent said patiently. 'Say you're a big manufacturer of toiletries and you were paying hundreds of thousands of dollars for a licence to market talcum powder, soap or whatever with Bubbles designs on the packaging and in your promotional material. You'd expect something unrecognisable from the genuine articles, wouldn't you? So would your customers, and as the licensee you could argue your business would be put at risk if they suspected they were getting something less.'

Cheryl wasn't totally convinced. 'I don't know,' she faltered. 'Big business operations are outside my experience, I'm afraid.'

'Sure,' Kent acknowledged. 'They're not my scene either. All I know is that it's a fickle world, and fame and fortune slip away very quickly for the silliest reasons. But maybe we can forget about that side of it for the moment. I've got something to show you.' He thrust a lean hand into an inside jacket pocket and produced a slim folder of photographs. 'Pictures of my island,' he said with simple pride, spreading half a dozen prints before her.

The colours were vibrant against the

whiteness of the tablecloth. The bright blues of clear skies and sparkling seas, and the verdant greens of lush, semi-tropical foliage fringed by clean sands matched anything Cheryl had ever seen in a travel brochure. And all this was his.

'They're lovely pictures,' she breathed in a small voice, and pointed. 'This aerial shot is breathtaking. It's the picture-book island paradise.'

Even in the soft illumination of the restaurant's chandeliers, the photographs gleamed as though with an inner light of their own.

'You're right,' he said. 'I'd never want to live anywhere else now. It uses up most of my income, of course, but it's worth every cent, and is a powerful motive for maintaining my output.' He sounded solemn in his sincerity.

'I can imagine,' Cheryl said dreamily. 'It would be a super place for a holiday.'

Kent looked suddenly disappointed. 'A holiday?' he said sharply. 'Do you mean you couldn't work there?'

'Oh, no,' Cheryl said, surprised by the intensity of his question. 'It's just that I thought . . . well, a permanent island lifestyle might not be just anybody's cup of tea.'

'The commitment would only be for two years,' he reminded her. 'And I've other staff on longer contracts — a housekeeper, a secretary, and a general handyman. So you wouldn't be completely lost for company, and the mainland is only minutes away by our sports cruiser.'

'A boat?'

'A marvellous boat. It's a fifteen-hundred-horsepower job and travels at fifty knots. Think of the isolation only as a means to privacy, and it can be very attractive.'

Cheryl sat there, ostensibly just looking at the pictures of the island. She saw them, but didn't see them. The time for stalling was over. She had to give this quietly insistent man a decision. The devil of it was she still hadn't made it, but if she spoke she would have done.

'Is there anything else you need to know?' he asked her kindly.

'No; it's all very impressive and well-organised, I'm sure . . . and . . . ' She ran out of pleasantries.

'Yes?' he encouraged her.

'And I want to accept the opportunity.' She said the fateful words in a rush, white-faced except for two flushed spots in her cheeks — and that could have been the wine.

Kent's craggy features broke in a broad smile. 'That's a huge relief,' he breathed. 'I'm sure you'll have nothing to regret.' He lifted her hand and squeezed it gently in a slightly formal handshake.

'I expect tomorrow I'll be filled with all sorts of qualms and remorse,' she said huskily.

The genuineness about her had impressed him from the start. 'It wouldn't be natural any other way,' he said, returning the direct gaze of her hazel eyes. 'But when it comes to signing the papers, I know you'll stand by your word. I don't have to take a chance on it.'

'You're right. The chance you're taking is on my talent and my ability to fit in on your island. Isn't it going to be difficult for you, too?'

'More difficult than you know,' he murmured mysteriously. 'But tonight let's just celebrate! I'm in the mood.'

His smiling enthusiasm pleased her. 'What exactly do you have in mind?' she asked, casual but cautious.

'A small club in Soho. Nothing disreputable. Good music, room to dance if it's not too crowded, and drinks that are what they're supposed to be.'

Oh, what a persuasive man he was! And all scarcely without trying. Cheryl could summon no objections. She wondered if he could guess how secretly proud she would feel just to be seen in his handsome company.

The Bayou was a swift taxi ride away, a cellar club down a steep flight of carpeted stairs lined with mirrors that made them seem wider than they were, if only a little. It pulsed with the sounds of New Orleans. A doorman built like a wrestler looked them over with steely eyes. Cheryl felt uneasy, but Kent produced a gilt-edged card from his wallet that acted like a magic talisman.

When they entered the club proper, the band was filing out for a break. Dancers were drifting back to tables and groups were gathering at the glittering bar.

Cheryl took up what might not be a long-lived chance for conversation. 'Do you come to places like this often?' she enquired.

Kent made a wry face. 'Hardly. You might say I've preferred to keep my own company over the past few years. But I like the music here. I don't care for passing fads. So when I'm in London, yes, this is one of the places I come.'

Did she detect a quiet bitterness in his tone? Cheryl reflected on the strangeness of him. He was a handsome, moneyed man at the top of his chosen tree. He was probably only in his mid-thirties, but he apparently lived the greater part of his life secluded like a hermit — although she had to concede the surroundings he'd picked looked idyllic.

The silence between them lengthened. Then Kent gave her a sideways glance. He couldn't see all he wanted, it seemed, and he swung round in front of her to look straight into her face, placing his hands on her shoulders. She was intensely aware of the warmth of them through the thin material of her dress.

'What's wrong?' he demanded. His face was half-shadowed and hard in the dim light.

She smiled uncertainly. 'Nothing . . . Shall we find somewhere to sit?'

His stiff hands relaxed and lifted. 'You'd gone very quiet. I thought you might have taken an instant dislike to the place.'

'It wasn't anything like that. I was just thinking.'

Kent smiled to himself and nodded. 'I thought so,' he said, contradicting what he'd said previously. 'You were wondering what you've let yourself in for, is that it?' He cupped one hand gently under her chin.

Cheryl felt colour tinge her cheeks. 'Something like that.'

'But not changing your mind already, I hope,' he probed. The hand cupping her chin opened and sensitive fingers brushed her cheek.

Cheryl jerked her head away. 'Of course not,' she said, as though stung by his suggestion. 'I understand what's involved, and I'm not the sort of person to go back on my word. You said so yourself.'

In fact, she was weirdly affected by his brushing touch. Her heart had surely missed a beat. Was he interested in more than just her work? She was suddenly scared of fooling herself; imagining things.

Kent appeared not to notice. 'Well, that's a relief! You had me worried for a moment. Come on, let's get ourselves some drinks. We're here to celebrate, remember?'

Cheryl had a premonition from then on that their coming to the Bayou would prove a mistake. She knew it from the pit of her stomach.

Kent didn't declare it, but he had the air of someone who'd cast a weight off his shoulders and was now determined to catch up with fun he imagined he'd missed before. Cheryl's whole mood was to the contrary. Her preference was for somewhere quiet, somewhere to take stock and get accustomed to the implications of a radical redirection in her life. She had more than her fair share of courage, but the thought of abruptly taking off for the other side of the world was something else. It loomed dauntingly in her mind. How could she do it? How could she possibly cope? And then there was her ridiculous notion that Kent Gordon could become more in her life than an employer. The moment when he'd touched her face and her heart had skipped a beat kept on disturbing her minutes later.

She sipped rum and Coke, and tried to relax. 'I suppose I shouldn't have come, really. I hate to be a wet blanket,' she apologised.

She wondered why she'd allowed herself to stumble into this commitment to celebrate. Couldn't she have turned his invitation down; made some conventional excuse? *I have a headache. I'm too tired.* It would have been so much easier. The more she examined her motives, the more fantastic they seemed. She was being cleverly lured by the promise of a huge reward and . . . what else? With a stab of alarm, it came home to her how easy it would be to have a crush on a stunning man with talent and a fortune; to be swayed by his probably casual attentions into accepting what might be unwise. But it was too late. Somehow, with his grand meal, his charming manners, and his pretty pictures, he'd already manipulated her into a momentous career decision she now felt compelled to abide by, even if she'd yet to sign the papers.

'You don't look very happy here,' Kent commented. 'What do you think I should have done? Taken you back to that cramped little flat to brood?'

'The flat's quite adequate as such places go, and I have Sue for company,' Cheryl said defensively.

'Of course,' he agreed. 'But Sue has a fiancé, and the flat is marked for demolition. You can't feel very secure there.' Did she hear a touch of scorn in his voice?

The band was returning to the raised platform that served as a stage. Cheryl twisted her hands together. 'Well,' she said, with a feeling of relief that this awkward conversation would soon be at an end, 'at least your plans for me solve my housing problem.'

Kent's jaw tightened as though

something in her tone of voice offended him. Their earlier rapport, it seemed, was already crumbling. Then a thumping piano, backed by guitar, bass, drums, and a lineup of saxophones, shattered any chance of comment.

Kent shrugged helplessly. He saw enough humour in the situation to let his face muscles loosen again. The beginnings of a smile tugged at the corners of his mouth. He leaned towards Cheryl. 'Shall we join the dancers?'

She rose to her feet mechanically, expecting not to do more than go through the appropriate motions. In the crowd and the dim light, she could give a passable imitation of enjoying herself. It would be enough to keep them inconspicuous, but not, she thought, to deceive Kent.

How wrong she was!

Once on the floor, the music and the dancing oddly proved therapeutic. The natural pleasure at being escorted by a dishy man who commanded wealth and fame reasserted itself. It took her out of herself. And her entire body trembled at the nearness of his.

When they left the floor, her cheeks were warmly flushed and her eyes shining. They weaved their way through the crowd, hand in hand.

'Kent!' exclaimed a voice close by. Startled, they looked round. 'It's been a year or two, but I can't believe you've entirely forgotten me!'

'Eileen . . . Eileen Dixon!' he greeted the woman.

'Ah, so you do still acknowledge an old workmate. I've been here ever since you arrived.'

'I'm sorry, I didn't notice you.'

But Eileen Dixon was the kind of person you did notice, Cheryl reflected. She was a large woman, thirtyish, with jet-black hair piled in an elaborately structured style on the crown of her head. She was flamboyantly dressed in a scarlet gown that matched the vivid red gash of her lipstick. Cheryl had noticed her out of the corner of her eye while they'd been dancing.

'Eyes only for your charming companion, obviously,' said Eileen archly. 'You must introduce me.'

'Of course — Cheryl Maitland, Eileen Dixon,' said Kent briskly, his face set in a stony mask. It registered with Cheryl that he was far from pleased.

Eileen was unabashed. 'I knew the exclusive Mr Kent Gordon before his rise to riches and fame,' she prattled to Cheryl. 'My sweet, the things I could tell you ... We worked for Popular Publications around the same time. He drew charming little funnies for kiddies' weeklies, and I worked as a very junior assistant on one of the women's rags in the same building.'

Her confiding manner grated with Cheryl. With strangers it was less than polite to be more than courteous. But Cheryl's reserve was lost on Eileen. She might never have noticed it. 'Now tell me, how do you fit into this gorgeous rich hunk's life?' she asked boldly.

Cheryl was stunned by her audacity, and Kent hurried to forestall the reply forming on her lips. 'Miss Maitland works for an advertising agency,' he said with a cold abruptness. 'I'm sure the details have no interest for you.'

Eileen scoffed. 'Come, come, Kent darling — you can't fob me off that easily. Why, you've not even half answered my question to Cheryl, and I'm quite sure she has a tongue in her own head.'

Kent looked as though he would like to wring Eileen's neck, and Cheryl knew he had not the slightest wish to renew their past acquaintance. It was time she spoke up. 'Look, Miss Dixon, I don't 'fit into' Kent's life. It's nothing like that at all. And neither of us is going to be around town for you to bother about much longer anyway.'

'Is that right?' Eileen probed slyly. 'Do you mean Kent is bolting back to that desert island of his so soon and — ' She broke off, as though struck by sudden illumination. 'No, don't tell me,' she breathed. 'And you are going with him!'

Cheryl stared straight back into her wide mascaraed eyes. 'As a matter of fact, yes,' she said defiantly.

'Well, well, this is a surprise. And tell me, my sweet, if you don't fit into Kent's life, what on earth will you be doing there?'

Cheryl realised too late that she'd let slip more than she'd intended. Her heart beat faster and she felt the palms of her hands go moist. Kent had been so insistent that she would work for him on a confidential basis. Now she was trapped into having to reveal the arrangement to this persistent, inquisitive individual who had the stamp of a gossiping socialite all over her brittle, enamelled façade. She groped in panic for words. She felt she could sense Kent's fury mounting, and it was he who spoke first in a forthright tone that brooked no argument.

'I can't see what business it is of yours, Eileen, but if you must know

Cheryl and I, though we've only recently met, are head over heels in love. We'll shortly be announcing our engagement. So it's thoroughly natural that she'll be going with me when I leave London.' He put a possessive arm round Cheryl and drew her tightly against him.

She was totally numbed. With Kent's earlier soft touches on her hands and shoulders, she had felt little surges of warmth, and a hint of excitement she had reflexively suppressed. This time she felt nothing but shock. What on earth was Kent saying? And why?

4

Reluctant Fiancée

Eileen was observing Cheryl with a strangely intent look, and Cheryl tried desperately to force a smile. A forthright person at heart, she didn't find the pretence easy.

Suddenly the evening had crashed around her ears. A few short minutes ago, she had felt good. Her qualms about coming to the Bayou had been beaten off, and she had been ready to feel on top of the world. Now this hideous woman had spoiled it all, somehow forcing Kent to say the craziest things. And she was expected to look as if nothing had gone wrong.

Fortunately, Kent still had his wits about him. 'Well, see you around, Eileen,' he said flatly. 'Cheryl is tired and we were about to leave anyway.'

Then he was striding away towards the stairs, towing her by the hand, limp and unresisting, in his wake.

In the taxi back to Cheryl's flat, Kent's fury subsided. 'I'm really sorry that had to happen, Cheryl,' he apologised. Then a gentle smile started to play around his lips. He was incredibly handsome. 'Thanks to a little subterfuge, that nosey moo will have been put right off the scent!'

'Yes, well, I can't exactly feel proud in condoning blatant lies, but she was a bit much,' Cheryl said, trying her best to sound cross.

During the journey, Kent arranged that Harvey Robinson's office would contact Cheryl to take care of the business arrangements for her new job and to set the date for her travel to New Zealand. 'I'll be going almost immediately, of course,' he informed her.

'Won't I be seeing you again, then?' she asked. The words were out of her mouth before her tired brain could properly consider what had prompted them, but she was vaguely aware of a sense of rejection.

'I can't see that it'll be necessary,' he said noncommittally. And when they alighted from the taxi outside Cheryl's flat, she felt deflated by his polite handshake.

She didn't look back as he returned to the cab, and she slotted her key into the front door. The rumble of the taxi's engine died away into the distance, and she was left alone with her inexplicable feelings of hurt and regret.

It had been quite a day. Whatever happened, it would have to be a milestone . . . the day she accepted a new and unusual job that was going to take her to the other side of the world and bring her more money than she had ever had in her life. Her head buzzed with the enormity of it all. It was just as well Sue was still out, because the inevitable post-mortem on her eventful evening with Kent Gordon would have taxed her to exhaustion.

Her previous restless night brought

its own compensation. She was afraid that she would lie awake mulling over the new developments, but instead she fell deeply asleep soon after putting her head on her pillow.

⋆ ⋆ ⋆

She knew nothing until a hand was shaking her and a voice was calling her name. 'Cheryl! Wake up, will you? Cheryl, come on — it's important!'

'Sue . . . ' she mumbled, forcing her eyelids apart. 'What is it? I haven't overslept, have I?'

'No, it's barely seven, but you've got a phone call.' Sue sounded exasperated.

'Phone call?' Cheryl repeated blankly.

'Yes! And I'm sure it's him, and he says it's urgent.'

Cheryl stumbled out of bed, groping for her dressing gown. 'This is ridiculous,' she murmured as she made her way to the phone. 'You must've made a mistake, Sue. Sure it's not a wrong number?'

But it was Kent Gordon, sure enough. When Cheryl heard the briskness in his voice, she was immediately positive, too, that something had put him out badly.

'Cheryl, have you seen this morning's *Globe*?'

She was taken aback. 'Look, I've only just been woken up. I haven't had time to read the paper!' She didn't mean to sound rude, but was ready to be terse.

Kent was conciliatory. 'Yes, yes, of course. Silly of me. Well, will you grab a copy soon and ring me back when you've read what's on page four?' He gave her his number and rang off.

Sue came to her elbow with a cup of coffee. 'What's bugging that man? What did you get up to last night, for heaven's sake?'

Cheryl ran a hand through her tousled hair. 'I don't know. He says I'm to see something in the *Globe*.'

'That's the paper we have . . . the one with Bubbles in.' Sue rushed to get it from outside the door at the top of the stairs that led to their flat.

'I don't think it's anything to do with his comic strip,' Cheryl hedged as she flicked through the first few pages. Then she stopped with a gasp.

Seeing her ashen face, Sue snatched the paper from her and read. 'You don't know what you did last night? But it says here Kent Gordon is about to become engaged to 'stunning young blonde advertising executive Cheryl Maitland'!' Sue's voice rose to a wail of despairing amazement.

'And it's all nonsense!' Cheryl protested. 'See this name here? She's behind it!' She pointed to the small box under the headline, at the top of the centre column. It contained the words 'By Eileen Dixon'.

Rapidly, Cheryl filled Sue in about the obnoxious person who'd inter-rupted her and Kent's visit to the Bayou club. Then they read the news story again. It was typical tabloid journalism, making great play on Kent

Gordon's wealth and fame, his island lifestyle, his handsome looks. Naturally it could say little about his unknown future 'bride', but it made up for it with material dredged from the paper's back files detailing Kent's earlier 'ill-starred' marriage that had ended three years ago in divorce. It finished with a pointer to the page on which its readers could see today's adventure of Bubbles.

With fumbling fingers, Cheryl reached for the phone and tapped out the number Kent had given her. He sounded less frantically anxious than when he'd called, but was still very concerned.

'If only I'd known!' he groaned regretfully. 'It seems this Dixon woman now earns her living as a freelance reporter, and she specialises in gossip pieces about what they call celebrities.'

Cheryl was impatient to set the record right. 'I hate to think what my family and friends will think when they read this,' she said. 'The paper uses your work. You must have some

influence there. Deny the report immediately and insist they publish a
correction!'

'It might not be that easy now,' Kent
prevaricated. 'I'll see what can be done,
but I suggest we meet with Robinson at
his office later today and plan a course
of action. I take it you won't be
changing your mind about the job?'

'Of course not,' Cheryl snapped. 'I'm
committed. I gave you my word, didn't
I?'

The sorry business didn't augur well
for her new life, but Cheryl was set in
her mind that Eileen Dixon's meddling
shouldn't wreck her big chance. She
arranged with Kent to call in at
Farringdon Road when she left work
that afternoon.

'What a mess!' she complained to
Sue when she'd hung up. 'I'm going
to have heaps of explaining to do at
work.'

'You'll be giving your notice anyway,'
said Sue practically. 'Just say the
paper's exaggerated and you're taking a

holiday in New Zealand or something.'

'Hmm . . . Fat chance people will believe that!'

'They probably will when tomorrow's *Globe* takes back its story.'

'I certainly hope so,' said Cheryl fervently.

Sue slapped her on the back. 'Come on, it could be worse. Supposing Kent Gordon was old and ugly?' She laughed. 'Myself, now, I could quite fancy being engaged to a handsome millionaire.' Then she added hastily, 'That is, if I wasn't marrying the nicest man in the world already!'

★　★　★

At the advertising agency, Cheryl endured a day of open ribbing and furtive whispers by her workmates. Most of them appeared to accept her explanations, and she contrived to turn aside the enquiries that had to do with her future work plans.

The coming appointment with Kent

and Robinson loomed large and continuously in her mind, assuming the awesome dimensions of a council of war. She wondered whether Kent had made contact with the *Globe*'s news editor yet, and what success he'd had in putting out the fire of Eileen Dixon's sneaky report.

By the time she reached the dingy Victorian building that housed Robinson's offices, Cheryl was tired and tense. The matronly secretary showed Cheryl into her chief's room. Kent was already there with the twitchy little grey man.

'Is everything sorted out?' Cheryl blurted anxiously in answer to their greetings.

Kent waved his hand. 'That's what we're going to do now. But first things first ... ' he said, and Robinson coughed and began shuffling papers on his desk.

'A signature here and here,' the agent indicated.

Cheryl gazed distractedly over the

two A4 sheets of closely spaced typescript, both in duplicate. She was no expert in contract law and she didn't have the means to hire someone who was. She took the ballpoint pen Robinson pushed towards her.

'I'll trust you,' she said to Kent, signing mechanically. Her mind was on other things. 'The newspaper report bothers me most. Have you seen them, Kent? Have you fixed it up?'

'I said I'd see what could be done, remember?'

Cheryl's heart sank. A grim suspicion began to harden inside her. 'You *have* told them the truth, haven't you?' she asked warily.

'Actually I've told them nothing,' Kent said doggedly. 'It's too late. The damage is done. Anything we say now would compound it and maybe ruin all our other arrangements.'

'But that Dixon woman's lies have to be retracted!' Cheryl stormed.

Kent clasped her upper arm. 'Cheryl, it can't be done,' he told her, emphasising every word.

She gaped at him incredulously, suddenly close to tears.

'Look,' he said, more gently now, 'they weren't really Eileen's lies. They were mine, and you were partly to blame for my having to tell them. We'll have to live with it, or scrap everything. We'd agreed how vital it was that the wider world shouldn't know you're going to be collaborating in my work. You can't now expect me to insist on having that truth emblazoned in the *Globe*.'

Cheryl shook her head and clenched her fists with frustration. Everything Kent said was true. But deep in her heart she felt it was wrong: that something was still being kept hidden from her; that she'd been trapped.

'Very well,' she replied, swallowing hard. 'But what do I tell the people at work? My mother?'

'For the time being we'll have to go along with what was in the paper. There's no other way.'

Robinson was nodding in agreement. 'Quite, quite. We could accelerate your departure plans, my dear, and perhaps you could claim some sick leave from your present employers. I'm sure that under the circumstances they wouldn't insist on your working out your notice.'

'You two seem to have it all worked out,' Cheryl said shakily. 'I suppose you think in the long run it won't make too much difference for you. The poor girl will just have a broken engagement to live down along with her hundred thousand pounds!'

She thought she saw Kent wince at the bitterness in her voice, then his expression softened and he stepped closer and put an arm around her comfortingly. 'I'm sorry,' he said with simple sincerity. 'I truly am. I never thought it could become so painful, but it'll all be behind us once we catch that plane for New Zealand, I'm sure.'

For just a moment, in the protective circle of Kent's arm, Cheryl wondered what it would be like if she were in truth his fiancée, and not merely condemned to act a role. Then the enormity of what she was daring to think caused her to shudder; and Kent, perhaps misinterpreting her reaction as aversion, released her quickly and moved away to Robinson's desk.

'Suppose I want to change my mind,' Cheryl said. On an impulse she stepped after him and reached towards the papers she'd signed. But Kent snatched them up almost from under her fingertips. He looked at her, hard-faced and challengingly.

'Yes . . . ?' he prompted her.

'Yes! You've tricked me. I didn't agree to go to your island as your fiancée, did I?'

Kent quirked an eyebrow and made as though to read the contract, though it was clear to Cheryl he already knew every word and punctuation mark on the papers.

'And you still haven't,' he told her blandly. 'But you have assigned to us sole rights in any cartoon work you do for the next two years.'

Cheryl gasped. 'In other words, if I want to pursue my ambition I'm compelled to work for you, like it or not?'

'That's about it. It's not so bad, is it? Work for would-be comic-strip artists is far from plentiful like in past times. The kids' comics you had your eye on are a sector of a publishing industry in worrying decline.'

'I know that!' Cheryl retorted. 'But it's not the point.'

'Not *the* point, but *a* point. With many thousands of pounds in the mix, it should have a strong financial bearing.' He thrust the papers at Robinson. 'Here, Harvey. I think you'd better lock these safely away.'

Anger glimmered in Cheryl's watching eyes. 'You think you've won, don't you? Well, all right. I'll go along with the contract. You've pointed out before that it suits me to, given my changing circumstances. But I warn you now, I'll be looking after myself, and I won't shrink from getting to the bottom of your schemes.'

Kent inclined his head — mockingly?

'You'll be told all you need to know,' he stated gruffly. 'For the meantime, all I ask you to do is go along with the general plan to lie low while airline tickets are bought and the necessary New Zealand entry documents arranged. I trust you won't wish to object to that?'

'Don't patronise me!' Cheryl snapped. 'Of course not. You've already made things embarrassing enough. I would hardly choose to draw extra attention to myself.'

Robinson promised meekly, 'It shouldn't take too long. As little as a week, if we can pull the right strings.'

A week, and her future for two whole years would be settled! A week, and she would be saying goodbye to her flatmate and home of the past eighteen months. To replace it with what? Two years of growing friction in close proximity to a man who failed to keep his word and explained himself in exasperating half-riddles. To think she'd let his smooth charm trap her into signing papers that practically made her his captive!

That night she forced herself to telephone her mother.

'You should have rung before,' her mother complained. 'It's just as it ever was — no consideration. You should be ashamed of yourself that I should've had to read about it first in a newspaper. Your Dad, too.'

'He's not my re — ' Cheryl began and then checked herself. Her relationship with her stepfather was old ground she'd been over countless times before. She saw it now with startling clarity for what it was — petty and no longer of any significance.

'How I'll be able to hold up my head before the neighbours, I don't know,' her mother prattled on. 'My daughter getting engaged to a man I've hardly heard of and never seen.'

There was more protest of a similar kind, much more. Cheryl resigned herself to listening and steeled herself not to answer back as her mother got into her familiar stride and threw her fit. On this occasion it wasn't too hard, because many of the things Cheryl heard put into words her own deepest reservations and fears. She was fleeing with the scantiest of consideration to a far-off corner of the world with a none-too-clear scheme of furthering a wild ambition. (To her mother all ambitions to do with art were 'wild'.) What was more, she was doing it with a man whom apparently she scarcely knew.

'It's almost indecent!' her horrified mother fumed. 'The only mercy your dad and I can see in the whole business is that he plans to marry you.'

'You poor thing,' Sue sympathised when Cheryl finally escaped from the phone, drained.

It was only the first of a series of harrowing days during which Cheryl was frequently obliged to hold her peace while her natural desire was to do the opposite. Often she yearned to speak out, to explain, to correct others' erroneous assumptions. It was a huge trial. Only with trusty Sue, from whom she couldn't keep the pain hidden, could she share her troubles.

'I wonder if that man knows what he's putting you through,' her friend grumbled.

But whatever the other women at the ad agency said, Cheryl also knew they envied her. Their jibes forced to her to think about Kent all the time. At least, why else should his image be constantly in her mind? Without meaning to, she became fiercely defensive of him when they made their little criticisms of his fast work in rearranging her life.

'When will you be getting your ring, Cheryl?' emerged as one of the more persistent inquiries. She was betrothed to a rich celebrity, wasn't she? Her tormentors expected to see something breathtakingly extravagant and expensive.

Cheryl yearned to see Kent Gordon

again — so that she could clear up these bothersome forgotten details and reiterate her opinion of his underhanded tactics. But after the encounter at the Bayou, Kent was virtually confining himself to his hotel room, and he sent no invitation for her to call. He'd got what he'd wanted from her, it seemed, and had no inclination to hasten the commencement of what now threatened to be a less-than-harmonious association.

But almost as though telepathy had transmitted Cheryl's concerns, a package arrived by courier at her flat.

5

We Need to Talk

Curiously, Cheryl cut open the outer padded bag. Inside was a note and a small square box. Gilt script on the box spelled out the name of a very high-class jeweller's in Knightsbridge.

She opened it with trembling fingers, and cried out in wonder. Nestling in a cushion of red velvet was a scintillating diamond set on a thin gold band. She couldn't have been more stunned if the parcel had been a bomb, and was unable to stop herself sliding the ring onto her finger.

For a moment she could almost believe she was betrothed to Kent Gordon. A thrilling shiver rang through her. Scared by the inappropriateness of her reaction, she pulled off the ring and snatched up the note.

Dear Cheryl, it read. *We must be prepared to deal with all questions and eventualities. Clearly our reported engagement should be supported by the evidence. Therefore, please will you wear this ring? If it does not fit comfortably, let me know and I will arrange for it to be altered. Regards, Kent.*

'This is insane!' Cheryl said aloud to the empty flat. A real diamond engagement ring costing thousands of pounds . . . she couldn't accept it!

She rushed to the telephone and, disregarding an earlier vow, called Kent's hotel and asked to be put through to him. Immediately.

'Kent Gordon,' he answered, almost cautiously.

'Are you completely out of your mind?' she almost shouted at him.

'Who is this?' he asked sharply.

'Cheryl Maitland, of course!'

'Ah, I thought it must be,' he said calmly. 'What's the excitement now?'

'As if you don't know! I've got your

curt little note and the ring, that's what. And I think it's totally ridiculous and insulting. You're taking things too far!'

'Oh dear,' he said in apparent dismay. 'Harvey and I thought it would be unwise to rely on half-measures. The note explains, and I don't know what you mean by curt. It's only like a business memo, after all.'

Was it the words 'only a memo' or her powerlessness that caused tears to prick her eyes? 'But a much cheaper ring would have been enough . . . ' she moaned in disbelief.

'Now come on,' Kent soothed. 'What sort of scrutiny would that stand up to? A man of substance can't give his fiancée a cheap ring.'

She couldn't contest his argument. 'I hate the thought of having to wear it,' she maintained sullenly. But the moment she'd said the words, she remembered guiltily the automatic pleasure it had given her to slide such beauty on to her finger.

'You've *got* to wear it, though,' he

insisted quietly. 'It's not so distasteful a thing to do, surely?'

'I'll be glad when it's over.'

'And it soon will be,' he promised her. 'Once we get to New Zealand and my island, you can chuck the ring in the sea for all I care. I shan't ever need to go to the mainland with you, so we won't be seen together, and there'll be no one to recognise you by yourself.'

For that, Cheryl could find no reply. Pangs of regret for making the hasty call knifed through her. 'Very well then, I go along with it, I suppose.'

'Fine. Let's forget all about this conversation.'

Cheryl put the receiver down gingerly, as though it had suddenly become dynamite. She had never felt so incapable of dealing with the emotions swirling within her.

It was time to make a new resolve: to get things in perspective before she drove herself mad.

★ ★ ★

Cheryl stayed on at the flat until the last possible moment. Sue had brought forward her plans to move back in with her parents until her marriage to Mike, but she was to see out a last week there, taking care of the final tidying up and disposing of those odds and ends of domestic equipment she and Cheryl would no longer need.

'Don't come to the airport, please,' Cheryl begged her. 'I might do something silly like burst into tears. So it would be much nicer to say our goodbyes here.'

In the event it was as well they did, because happenings at Heathrow contained some unwelcome surprises.

Cheryl and Kent had just got out of their taxi, and their baggage was being loaded onto a trolley to be taken to the airline's reception point, when suddenly another car squealed to a halt behind the cab. Two people jumped out. One was a lanky middle-aged man in slightly scruffy clothes. A bulky bag swung from his shoulder, and he was armed with a professional-looking camera held at the ready. The other was Eileen Dixon. She wore loosely cut trousers and a bright green nylon jacket, and, clutching a spiral-bound notebook, looked ready for business.

'Oh, damn!' Kent cursed in Cheryl's ear. 'I might have expected this, but it's just what we don't need!' He put his arm round her protectively as they rounded to meet the brazen scribbler. Cheryl felt herself go tense all over.

'Hello, darlings!' Eileen gushed. 'I see I'm just in time. Now what about some parting words from our favourite cartoonist and his blushing bride-to-be?'

Cheryl cringed. The temptation to tell this overbearing busybody to get lost was strong, but she bit her tongue as she knew she must.

Kent laughed dismissively. 'I thought you'd already told the whole story quite well without any help from us.'

'A picture, then!' Eileen whirled on Cheryl. 'How about a lovely close-up of that super rock on your finger, my sweet?' she cooed.

The tall, scruffy man lifted his camera and sighted it on Cheryl's hand. Reflexively she stiffened and drew back.

'Ah, the little girl's bashful, Ted. Perhaps her man can be persuaded to hold her a teensy bit closer? Come on, Kent, love, give her a cuddle now!'

To Cheryl's horror, Kent complied, and the camera flashed. How far would this charade go?

Eileen already had her plans there. 'Now then, Kent, a kiss for your fiancée! We can't settle for less!' The words dripped from her overpainted lips like warm treacle, turning Cheryl's stomach to one heavy lump of anger. She could hardly breathe, her chest was so tight.

'Well, if you insist, Eileen,' Kent said lightly. 'It would be less than gallant to refuse . . . '

Cheryl was afraid to turn her face to him, and she was sure her cheeks must be flaming. But then she felt his fingers, strong and slender, on her chin, turning her head towards him. His eyes met hers and seemed to speak. 'It's only a pretence,' they were saying. 'We needn't feel anything.'

She started to relax. It wouldn't be so bad. He understood. The kiss would be a perfunctory one, just enough for them to get these horrible people out of their hair and to escape into the waiting hall.

She closed her eyes and his head lowered towards her, then his lips brushed hers hoveringly. There, it was over! But no — suddenly his lips returned, differently now, seeking urgently with an unmistakable passion. They came down hungrily on hers.

Without warning, a fire ran through her, intense and overwhelming. Her senses were consumed and she answered his kiss shamelessly with a stifled moan. In that moment nothing mattered except the fiery glow of pleasure sweeping her from head to toe.

Dimly she was conscious of a pop of

light from the pressman's camera, and abruptly it was over. Kent had released her and she was at arm's length, her eyes open to a rigidly smiling face which she could have sworn was a mask for amazed disbelief. Her head swam as though she had just stepped off a fairground roundabout.

'Bravo!' applauded the obnoxious Eileen in a world returning from somewhere far away. 'That's the stuff to give 'em. The readers love a sexy picture!'

It broke the spell, filling Cheryl with remorse. Wildly, she weighed her chances of grabbing the lanky man's camera and smashing it to the ground. But that was being naive. A scene like that could only compound her embarrassment, and already their baggage was being trundled away and Kent was turning to follow, tugging her after him by the hand.

'Bye, Eileen,' he said. 'See you again not too soon, I hope. And don't say I never do you favours.'

'Huh!' the gossip writer scoffed. 'The fun you were having just then, it looked to me like I was doing you two the favour!' Her scruffy companion sniggered as he packed his camera into his bag.

'Grrr, she's an insufferable woman!' Kent muttered through his teeth as they went inside. 'It's a miracle someone hasn't strangled her.'

He led Cheryl in a daze through the formalities of checking in for their flight. But by the time they were seated in the departure lounge, waiting for their flight to be called, she had recovered most of her shattered faculties and pieced them carefully back together.

'Kent,' she said severely, mustering her confidence, 'will you put that newspaper down? I think we've got to get things straightened out, don't you?'

'Mm . . . what was that you said?' he asked, lowering his paper with a conspicuous rustle.

'I think we need to talk before we go any further.'

'You do?' he said innocently. 'About what?'

'About us. About what happened just then. This — this masquerade can be taken a bit too far, you know.'

'You mean I kissed you for the benefit of Eileen Dixon's silly games?'

'Exactly. And it seemed to me we got a bit carried away. I'm only going through with this contract of ours because I have to, and we can't afford to let that kind of thing get in the way. The engagement is only a pretence after all, isn't it? I'm coming to your island solely because I'm compelled to if I want to work as a cartoonist.'

He laughed with a sudden flash of cynicism in his eyes. 'Of course! But it has to be a good pretence for the likes of a hardened old yellow-press journo like Eileen. Don't tell me you were taken in, too?'

Cheryl shrivelled up inside, mortified at having betrayed her own indiscretion.

'Oh . . . then it really did mean nothing to you?' he pressed.

'Of course it didn't. You're worrying your head about nothing. There's no way I'll get carried away, as you put it. I've been down that road before, you know. My drawing is the only thing that really matters.'

He leaned forward and patted her hand, almost paternally. 'Once we get to New Zealand, we can drop and forget this whole stupid game. You'll see — we'll get things on to a strictly work-only footing. There won't even be time for hanky-panky, let alone any need.'

Cheryl lifted her head and nodded. 'Good,' she returned, trying to sound grateful for his reassurance. 'That's very . . . comforting to know.'

But an unconquerable spark deep inside told her she was a hypocrite, and that for some reason she should be feeling deeply hurt.

The same voice also said it was convinced Kent was lying about his feelings, too. But why, it didn't know.

6

Journey's End

'Look!' said Kent Gordon. 'Your first sight of Aotearoa, as the Maori call it — the land of the long white cloud.'

Cheryl roused herself from a doze. Could they really be over New Zealand at last? The journey had been tiring and trying, particularly the last leg from Sydney. A home-going rugby team had spent an hour or more shouting and laughing and whooping before the liquor they consumed in astonishing quantities began to produce an anaesthetic effect. Before that, she'd been bored by the in-flight movies and niggled by Kent's cool reserve. And having a window seat had its drawbacks, too. She didn't like to keep climbing over people to reach the aisle, so exercise between the interminable meals — for which, too nervous to eat, she could only summon the appetite to pick at — had been limited.

Now the window seat could offer its advantages. The airliner was banking slightly. Kent pointed with his lean brown artist's hand. Through the parting cloud, across the aircraft's wing, and past an engine pod, Cheryl glimpsed a white-edged green land set in a brilliant blue sea.

It was more than twenty hours since they'd left London, but the weight of travel fatigue lifted from her slender body. She wriggled up in the seat and brushed aside a stray wisp of russet hair to clear her view. 'Oh, it's wonderful,' she breathed, unable to suppress her appreciation.

'A green and pleasant land, truly,' said Kent. 'But like everywhere, it has its problems and difficulties from time to time, especially in the cities. Fortunately, Cabin Island is well away from them.' At last a note of enthusiasm crept into his voice, lessening the tension that had lain between them during the incredibly long journey. 'The island has no law-and-order troubles, no nine-to-five rat race ... It's an idyllic place.'

Cheryl shook her head in wonder. 'To an ordinary person like me, who's lived in England all her life, the idea of a privately owned island is amazing — like something out of an old Enid Blyton novel.'

Kent laughed. 'It's true well enough. There are more than two hundred islands around the northern half of New Zealand's North Island. Some are little more than barren rocks, but about a third could be habitable. You're right about the private ownership, though. Most of them are crown property — or at least they're in the hands of various maritime park boards answerable to the government.'

'And your fortune has let you buy one of the others and keep it all to yourself.' She felt a return of resentment towards him. 'You have everything your own way, don't you?'

He shot her a reproving glance. 'You jump to too many conclusions,' he accused her.

'Oh really,' Cheryl returned with a brittle laugh, determined to hold to her chosen course of criticism.

'Yes, you're a bit wide of the mark. My earnings let me keep the island, but it was my grandfather who had the foresight to buy the place years and years ago, when it cost not much more than the price of a new car. Today wealthy people the world over hanker after such retreats — Americans, Europeans, Asians . . . it really is multi-millionaire territory.'

Cheryl was awed into silence. She could have bitten off her tongue for making the snide remark. It was nearly true, she felt sure, but the timing was inappropriate. Her intelligence should have warned her she was skating on thin ice. She'd had far too little knowledge of what she was ostensibly commenting on.

The feeling that she was stepping into an unfamiliar, strange new life grew as the airliner went through the routine that brought them down to earth at Auckland International Airport: the imperative flash of the seat belt light; the soft jolt as the wheels touched the runway; the roar of braking jets; the taxiing that brought them to the terminal building. In addition, the queues through immigration and customs seemed to delay them interminably. Kent accepted it all stoically, while Cheryl's impatience grew amid the irritated murmurs of fellow travellers and the wails of fractious children.

'Oh, I do wish they'd hurry up,' she said tiredly.

'When you've been through it a few times, you learn how to take it in your stride,' said Kent casually. 'Here, what do you think of this one?'

He had been sketching with a felt pen in the blank space of an advertisement on the back page of a magazine he carried. Cheryl saw he had caricatured the grim-faced immigration official awaiting them at the head of the queue. Despite herself, she chuckled. 'It's very clever!'

She instantly regretted the admission. Paradoxically, she felt less fearful when the truce between them was more fragile.

'I thought that might bring a smile to your face,' Kent said with quiet satisfaction. His contradictory behaviour was maddening.

'Well, you don't have to put me at my ease, and you don't have to impress me,' she disabused him swiftly.

'Oh, no?'

'No! You've got your signed pieces of paper safely locked away, haven't you? And you've made it ruthlessly clear that our association is to be nothing more than a business arrangement.'

'Does business have to be done in total bad humour?' he mused. 'I should have thought not.'

Nor were Cheryl's tribulations over.

Customs was especially crushing. Having Kent at her elbow doubled the embarrassment of watching an official riffle through her neatly packed underwear and toiletries. She felt ridiculous and exposed.

Then at last their bags were approved and they were free. In the arrivals hall they were met by Dean McBride, the son of Kent's housekeeper. He was in his late twenties, Cheryl guessed; a solid-looking fellow with a weather-beaten, dark-browed face and massive shoulders. He tossed their bags into the open boot of a waiting BMW as though they were filled with feathers.

'Dean is my chauffeur, boatman, groundsman, handyman, and a whole lot else,' Kent explained. 'A Jack of all trades.'

'Do we have far to go?' Cheryl asked with brusque weariness when they were ready to leave.

'We'll be in the car for about three hours,' Kent informed her dryly. 'But I'll travel in the front with Dean, so feel free to make yourself at home in the back. You can stretch out and have a doze, if you like. Dean is a very competent driver and the car is quiet and comfortable.'

Far from feeling grateful, his solicitude left Cheryl with a sensation that she'd been rejected. After travelling across the world by her side, he obviously couldn't wait to cast her off for other company! Again, she reflected that life on his 'idyllic' island could become a lot more trying than she'd anticipated.

She sat in silence as the powerful car weaved through suburban turnings, then gathered speed and suddenly merged into the traffic travelling north on a motorway.

Kent and Dean talked about practical things that tacitly excluded her — modifications to an electricity generator, plans to clear some noxious weeds, whether a desalinator should be added to the equipment on Kent's luxury boat.

Before long the road was curving across a flyover, then through a short tunnel down to a waterfront with big houses perched on low cliffs to the left and scores of expensive yachts bobbing in a boat harbour to the right. Ahead, the silver span of the Auckland Harbour Bridge soared across the sparkling waters. From the top of the bridge, Cheryl was momentarily able to marvel again at the beauty of Kent's homeland. Behind them, to the right, was a city of shimmering white office and hotel towers interspersed with the green-clad cones of long-dead volcanoes. To the left, the city development gave way to suburbs and rolling green hills. Before them were estuaries and mangroves fringing a second set of built-up communities on the harbour's other shore.

Already Cheryl had noticed the mixture of English and Maori place names on the white-on-green road signs erected on gantries across the motor-way lanes. All around her was a mixture of the oddly familiar and the tantalisingly strange. She hoped that sometime during or after her enforced exile on Cabin Island she would be able to visit and explore these places. But then her spirits plunged. It struck her that she would be very much the stranger in a strange land. Kent Gordon was the only person she knew here, and it was just dreaming to think he might want to show her round the tourist sights.

Cheryl slumped down in her seat, feeling misused and cheated. The arrangement she'd allowed herself to be conned into had scarcely begun, but already the situation was almost beyond bearing.

Eventually Auckland was left behind and, with the motorway ended, the car was travelling on a narrower, winding road that led to the north. Kent leaned back and gave her a grin. 'They call this State Highway One. A grand name, isn't it? In most places outside the developing world it would probably count as a country lane.'

So he hadn't entirely forgotten she was there, Cheryl thought moodily. But though his voice was light and friendly, he turned round again immediately and resumed his discussions with McBride.

They had been travelling now for an hour, which meant they would be on the road for two more. Cheryl decided she might do worse than take up Kent's suggestion that she should snatch some sleep. It was a joy to be able to kick off her shoes and stretch out in comfort after the cramped confines of a seat on an aircraft. She hadn't realised how tired the long flight had left her. Overcome by fatigue and her imponderable misgivings, she slept.

*   *   *

'I've got to wake up . . . I must wake up.' The message was drumming through her subconscious. Over and over it repeated itself, but she couldn't lift the immense weight of her head, and her eyelids felt glued together.

Did it really matter? How much easier it would be if this sleep could stretch on forever. What a blissful escape from a reality that had slipped out of her control, ringing her round with the daunting, sheer faces of a nameless pit.

But the thrumming of the tyres on the tarseal had changed its pitch. Her centre of gravity was being — for all the comfort of a top-class European car — thrown from one side to another, which unsettled her stomach to the point of queasiness. It was the thought that she would embarrass herself further by being car-sick that jolted her awake. The car was on a twisting, descending road bordered by steep red clay banks and dense greenery.

Kent noticed her movement. 'Feeling better, Cheryl?' he asked.

'Not really,' she answered honestly. She brushed back errant strands of reddish-brown hair with an unsteady hand, and in the driving mirror caught a glimpse of a red mark on her cheek where it had rested against the cushions. God, what a mess she must look, and how she hated the thought of that.

'Do we have far to go?' she said, trying to make an anxious enquiry sound nonchalant.

'Just minutes now. You've been asleep ages, but the last leg of the journey should clear the cobwebs.'

'That sounds a bit ominous.'

Kent laughed. 'Nothing to worry about at all! You'll enjoy it — won't she, Dean? And I think I can guarantee you'll never have travelled as fast on water as you will in the *Tigress*. We'll rocket out to the island at more than fifty knots.'

'How much is that in miles per hour?'

'Maths isn't my strong point, but I'd say between fifty and sixty, which on water is going some. What would you say, Dean?'

Dean grunted. 'It's awesome stuff all right. Them twin Chevys turn out fifteen hundred horsepower. That makes us almost as powerful as a railway locomotive.'

Cheryl swallowed. 'I think I'll have to close my eyes.'

'What!' Kent cried in mock indignation. 'Surely you'll want to see my beautiful boat?'

And see it she did, not less than ten minutes later when the road curved sharply and came to an end beside a general store and service station. Beyond the buildings was a slipway and an extensive concrete wharf on the shore of a broad estuary. The *Tigress* stood out among the many small vessels bobbing in the sheltered waters. It was painted black and yellow and stood out for both its size and sleek, sporty lines. Cheryl guessed it to be a little less fifty feet long and maybe fifteen feet wide.

A mature woman dressed somewhat incongruously in a crisp white blouse and dark skirt came onto the *Tigress*'s deck as they approached. 'Miss Rimmer came over with me to go into town to do some business,' Dean explained.

'Lois Rimmer is my local business manager and PA,' Kent told Cheryl. 'She looks after all the banking, pays the tradesmen, sees to correspondence, et cetera. Mrs McBride, Dean's mother, handles the domestic side of running the household.'

'It sounds very well organised,' Cheryl commented.

'It has to be, and it is. My staff are the last word in efficiency. That's why I employ them.'

Striving to keep any trace of nervousness out of her face, Cheryl wondered how she would fit into this team, and whether she would reach the high standards required. Well, Kent had virtually forced her to come. He'd get what he deserved, no more and no less!

They went down a short flight of stairs and stepped onto the boat's deck, where Cheryl was introduced to Lois. Everything about the woman struck Cheryl as being severe — the cut of her clothes, her voice, the dark hair drawn tightly into a French plait and streaked with strands of grey. Her gaze was penetrating. Without a word she contrived to say that she was not happy with what she saw in Cheryl.

'So you're Miss Maitland,' she acknowledged coolly. 'I understood from Harvey Robinson you were coming, and I think you'll find everything has been got ready for you on the island.'

At Kent's request Lois showed Cheryl below decks. She was astonished at the spaciousness of the accommodation and the quality of the fittings and furnishings. There was a galley, complete with fridge-freezer and hot and cold running water; and two cabins, the largest of which was equipped with stereo, video and — to Cheryl's sudden and odd embarrassment — a double bed fully six feet wide. After enduring the broom-cupboard-size toilets of the aeroplane that had brought her to New Zealand, the ample bathroom facilities were a joy she could appreciate immediately.

As she emerged onto the deck to rejoin the others, she caught the tail end of a conversation between Lois and Kent. 'But I didn't quite realise that she would be such a very young person . . . '

From their abrupt silence at her appearance, she surmised that Lois's words had been about her. They didn't help her feel comfortable — in fact, she resented them. So Lois thought she was too young. But for what? she might ask.

A sudden gust of the offshore breeze rattled through the rigging of nearby yachts, bringing a hint of the oncoming chill of evening. 'Let's make a move then, shall we?' Kent said. He went to the controls and pressed a button. The *Tigress* responded with a throaty roar. Then they were casting off and manoeuvring away from the wharf.

Cheryl felt the restrained throb of power as they nosed down the estuary, picking their way through the countless small boats moored in the stream. Several, she noticed, carried the names of foreign home ports on their sterns, like Amsterdam and San Francisco.

Lois came up quietly beside Cheryl. 'What a magnificent ring!' she observed.

Cheryl had been completely absorbed in the passing scene and did not instantly register that Lois was looking at her left hand where it rested lightly on the rail. 'Oh, yes, isn't it?' she flustered, reddening in her confusion.

'Do you wear it when you're working? I should think it would get horribly in the way.'

Behind them Kent chuckled. 'Cheryl isn't a southpaw like you, Lois. She's conventional and draws with her right. But later on I'll tell you about that ring. There's quite a story behind it.'

'I'm sure there is,' Lois murmured meaningfully. 'It looks incredibly expensive for a young artist.'

The thought of Kent explaining to Lois Rimmer about Eileen Dixon and the elaborate deception they'd been forced to practise in London struck Cheryl as positively hateful. It reminded her of how Kent had told her she could throw the ring in the sea when they reached their destination. And that hurt — not just a little, but very deeply. She tried to fathom why. Could it be the revelation that when things — even precious things — had been used and served their purpose, Kent had no qualms about discarding them? It was chilling to think this might apply to people, too.

7

Quarrel in the Night

Once the *Tigress* had emerged from the drowned river system into more open waters, Kent let her off the leash, and she sprang forward with a mighty howl of power. Spray whipped back from the bow as she carved through the waves. Behind them a creamy wake set up enormous, ever-spreading waves of its own across the sparkling serenity created by the setting sun.

It was an exhilarating experience. But Cheryl was puzzled by the harsh set of Kent's features. He drove his boat as though working out some deep anger or frustration to which he could legitimately give no other expression so violent. She thought about it for several minutes but could see no obvious explanation. Maybe she was being fanciful, she concluded. After all, she was very tired, and under stress herself.

After about fifteen minutes, a dot appeared on the horizon directly ahead. It grew rapidly, taking on the shape of a humpbacked island in shades of green — the dark of tree cover, the light of pasture. In places its shore was rocky, but in others it was fringed by white sands. The low sun tinged the sea, and the island looked like an emerald cast upon a rumpled sheet of shot silk in colours of purple and gold.

As Kent throttled back the engines, the twin fans of spray at the *Tigress*'s bow subsided, and the slap and hiss of the onrushing waves abated. The sleek cruiser purred towards a jetty that extended from the foot of a gentle green hill crested by a palatial bungalow above an old citrus orchard.

'Here we are, Cheryl ... Cabin Island, and every bit as pretty as those photos I showed you in London, don't you think?'

'It's overwhelming!' Cheryl breathed.

Whatever reservations she might have had about the bizarre adventure she'd embarked upon, there was no denying the picturesque island fulfilled every claim he had made about it. 'So very beautiful, Kent.'

'Well, that's high praise indeed from such a particular young woman as yourself.'

Cheryl fixed him with a look, searching for a trace of sarcasm to go with his words. But Kent was already occupied with the next claim to his attention. He deftly swung the *Tigress* parallel to the jetty, killing the engines, and Dean jumped onto the boards with a mooring rope.

A deep peace seemed to enfold them as the boat came to rest and rocked gently in its own wash rebounding from the shore. All that could be heard was the distant cry of sea birds, the gurgle of water swirling around the hull and the jetty's wooden piles, and the muffled breaking of the waves on the nearby shore. And these were little more than the sounds of silence.

An easy shingle track zigzagged up to the hilltop bungalow. Its walls reflected the warm pink of the evening sky, but Cheryl could see that they were painted no colour at all. Cedar planks had been left to weather naturally, making it at one with the landscape.

The housekeeper, Moira McBride, was waiting for them just inside the main entrance. She was a plump, rosy-cheeked woman. That and the apron she wore stamped her as a housekeeper in the traditional mould. Her kindly looks reminded Cheryl of a picture she'd seen in a nursery-level storybook she'd forgotten she'd ever had.

The arrivals stepped into a wide hallway paved with lichen-toned terra-cotta tiles.

'Welcome home, Mr Gordon! Let me look at you now,' fussed Mrs McBride. 'Come through and sit down. And Miss Maitland — it is Miss Maitland, isn't it? — you too, love. You must both be tired after all that flying.'

Cheryl mentally saw an absurd image of Kent and herself cleaving Peter Pan-style through the skies from London to Auckland.

Something of the sort must have occurred to Kent, too. 'The wings worked well, Moira,' he quipped. 'We aren't too weary, though Cheryl has been a little sleepy.'

'I think I'm a bit jet-lagged, that's all,' Cheryl said briskly. Why did Kent have to make what sounded like excuses for her?

Mrs McBride lightly clapped her hands together. 'A cup of tea and a light supper perhaps. Then an early night. But first I'll show you your room.'

In fact it was Kent who led the way. 'The layout looks confusing at first, but it's quite simple really,' he explained.

The main living rooms opened off the entrance hall — lounge, dining room, library, and Kent's workroom. This block of rooms formed the base of a U-shaped plan, and passages from the hall gave access to the two arms. One of these wings contained the kitchen and laundry and a storage area; the other was bedrooms. The centre of the U was taken up by a paved patio with shade trees and an ornamental pond and fountain. Cheryl's impression was of space and luxury.

She was shown to a guest room. 'I hope you'll find it comfortable,' Mrs McBride fussed. 'There's extra pillows in the top of the clothes closet should you want them, and your bathroom's just through here.' She opened a sliding door to a well-appointed little room, its walls half-tiled, then papered in the same design as the bedroom — a pale green dotted with yellow bell-shaped kowhai flowers. But what drew Cheryl's wondering eyes was a glass shelf crowded with exquisite cut-crystal decanters and bottles of perfumes and bath salts. All the items appeared expensive, unopened, and brand-new.

'Are they for me?' she asked incredulously.

Kent answered from the bedroom
behind her. 'Of course. I ordered them
specially. I thought you might like a few
extras to make your life here more
pleasurable.' He tossed the explanation
off lightly.

Cheryl was dumbfounded. 'I can't
accept them!' she blurted.

He shrugged as though her ingrati-
tude was of no account. 'I can't see
whyever not. But think about it. We can
always get Mrs McBride to remove
them if they're not to your taste.'

Reminded of the housekeeper's
presence, and becoming aware of her
puzzlement, Cheryl instantly regretted
her outburst. She made no effort to
pursue the matter, but she couldn't for
the life of her figure out Kent's
motives. The gifts were generous,
lavish, thoughtful . . . and quite at
variance with his professed attitude of
indifference to her beyond the bounds
of her contract. Once again, she had

the suspicion that Kent was hiding truth, and that he'd responded to a spontaneous desire that had somehow caught him out. Or was she being imaginative? It could just as likely be a piece of one-upmanship; a gesture to flaunt his wealth and power and subtly remind her that her comfort rested on his whim.

On legs curiously wobbly, Cheryl stepped back into the bedroom. Here the floor was fitted with thick carpet in a similar pale green to the wallpaper; and tinted windows, including a ranch-slider, opened on to the central patio. 'The room looks lovely,' she said, feeling chastened. 'I'm sure it'll meet all my needs.' In truth, she was once again overwhelmed. In all her life she'd never had so grand a place to call her own. And quite apart from the startling gifts, the idea of a bathroom, complete with shower, all to herself was simply unreal.

Then it was back to the others in the dining room for Mrs McBride's light supper. Cheryl gave her full attention to a mushroom omelette, some salad, and a small portion of cheesecake. But she felt far from at home in the unfamiliar surroundings. She almost wished she were back on the plane, eating off a plastic tray, with just Kent by her side. Fortunately the McBrides, Lois, and Kent made no attempts to draw her into their conversation — or, worse, to interrogate her, which she would have found unbearable.

Escape was not difficult. 'If you'll excuse me, I'm very tired. I should like to go to my room now — if that's all right with the head of the table.' She cast an enquiring glance meaningfully in Kent's direction.

'Sure,' he said with a nod. He hadn't risen to the edge she'd tried to put in her voice. On the contrary, he looked mildly amused and smiled at her irritatingly. 'Sounds a pretty good idea to me. I aim to get some shuteye myself shortly.'

Suddenly, in her room, Cheryl was at last alone. She pulled the cord that drew the curtains, peeled off her embroidered linen blouse and polished cotton jeans, kicked off her shoes, and with a huge sigh stretched herself out on the bed. It was just right — soft, but supporting. Within moments she was sinking luxuriously and unresistingly beneath a wave of drowsiness. But then she realised this would be folly in the long run, however tempting. What she needed to chase away her travel fatigue was a proper night's sleep. She'd had enough of cat naps and snatched dozes. So she forced herself to jump up, yawned and stretched, then went through to the bathroom to shower.

She revelled in the warm, cleansing spray. 'It's just what I needed,' she told herself. Now, a good night's rest and she would be a new person.

She towelled herself briskly and, after casting a guilty glance at the shelf of luxuries — which she hadn't touched, returned to the bedroom where she pulled her Bubbles nightdress case from her largest travel bag.

She hugged the toy to her still-damp body, but felt abruptly disturbed. Her attachment to the cuddly toy character was all at once bereft of its previous innocence. Her Bubbles was no longer hers. It was a creation of Kent Gordon's; it was forever the product of his imagination.

She was shocked by her own weird thoughts. What had brought about this sudden flood of emotionalism? It was unnatural and unwarranted. She searched her mind for a reason and found it at Heathrow. There, Kent had taken her in his arms and she'd felt a thrill of pleasure. But afterwards he'd rejected her concerns and been almost derisive. He'd made it humiliatingly clear that his own affections could not be engaged. All he wanted had been achieved when she'd foolishly trusted him and signed his ensnaring contract. How, then, could she dare to be affectionate towards Bubbles, who was part of him?

'Cheryl, you're being ridiculous!' she

reprimanded herself sternly. She quickly donned her nightdress and buried herself beneath the bedcovers as though she could hide from the nonsense that had entered her head.

The effort was doomed to failure, of course. She didn't want to lie there thinking fancifully about Kent Gordon. She didn't want to remember the abandonment of her senses when he'd kissed her. But it was impossible not to. It was folly, she argued to herself fiercely. He was attractive and talented and rich, but he was cold. How else could he have had no compunction about upsetting her life to serve his own desperate ends of deceiving Eileen Dixon and the world?

She was plagued with these insane thoughts for a whole hour before she reached a decision. This was enough! She would get dressed and take a walk outside to bring herself back to reality and perhaps put her mind in a better frame for sleep.

Thrusting back the covers, she

sprang out of bed and pulled on jeans and a warm sweater. She didn't like to go through the house — it wouldn't do to bump into the solicitous Mrs McBride or the watchful Lois Rimmer — so she pulled aside the curtains and went out through the ranch-slider onto the patio.

The night was warm, very clear and very still. She was amazed and thrilled by the sky. Never could she remember having seen so many stars, so bright and twinkling in every direction. The air on the patio was heavy with the strange scents of plants she could see only dimly and could not have named. In the semi-darkness the enclosed space reminded her of a cloistered quadrangle in an old-world convent or college, somewhere Mediterranean perhaps. The soothing patter of the fountain heightened the impression, yet an omnipresent whirr of cicadas and crickets was a counterpoint that would not let her forget the foreignness of her surroundings.

As her ears adjusted, filtering out the background cacophony, Cheryl became aware of voices. Someone else, too, was taking the evening air. Was it the McBrides . . . Lois . . . Kent? Or had some strangers landed on the island? Without knowing why, she was intensely curious. The voices pulled her like strings working the feet of a marionette. She followed a garden path that led from the patio round the side of the house to the track down the hill to the jetty and beach.

As she came to the front of the house, she saw that the other strollers were Kent and Lois. She was amazed at how far the sound of their voices had travelled, because they were down at the water's edge. Perhaps the contours of the land acted in some tricky way to amplify it. She thought it might be best to join them before they spotted her, and hurried down the track. Luckily their backs were turned to her as, almost before it was too late, she realised their voices were raised in vehement dispute. Embarrassed, on impulse she jumped off the track onto the beach and ducked into the shadows beneath the jetty.

'You can imagine my shock when I opened the paper and saw this!' Cheryl heard Lois say. There was a rustle of newspaper. 'I suppose you'd forgotten that news-agency photos go round the world instantly.'

Kent sighed wearily. 'Oh, I admit it, Lois, I had overlooked the fact. Who'd have thought Eileen Dixon's report and picture were going to be used so quickly here?'

'No wonder that girl was so cagey about the ring she wore. If only I'd had time to open this paper before the pair of you turned up at the boat!'

'Now that's rubbish! You would have said nothing, I hope. Like I said, it's just a hoax, a blind to keep the press off my back till my problem is fixed up.'

It was Lois's turn to sigh. 'I'm not so sure you've adopted the right tactics.

Her work looks good, I'll agree, but supposing she tries to take advantage of the situation?'

'For goodness sake, Lois!' Kent said. 'I've told you — I let her know the score. I'm not interested in her. In due course the 'engagement' will be broken off. And anyway, I don't think she's that kind of gold-digger.'

Lois scoffed. 'But she's young and impressionable. I can see all kinds of complications, I really can. I dislike this cloak-and-dagger nonsense intensely. It can't possibly improve your health.'

'Speaking of which, you'll be glad to know all this drama is bringing on a sick headache right now.'

'Oh, Kent!' Lois said with feeling. 'There's no need for that sarcastic tone. Come on, let's get back to the house. You know what the doctors said — avoid exertion and emotional stress at all costs.'

'I've not forgotten, Lois, I can guarantee you that; but whatever I do, it seems to become increasingly difficult. I solve one problem and another pops up in its place.'

Cheryl slipped behind a piling as the pair left the jetty to begin their way back to the house. They passed within an arm's reach of her.

'Kent, you are keeping up the medication, aren't you?' Lois asked. Her voice was edged with a desperate concern.

'Religiously,' he groaned. 'Night and morning.'

Cheryl twisted her hands together in anguish, not trusting herself to move an inch until their voices were a distant murmur and their shapes were swallowed up by the shadow of the house. What was 'this cloak-and-dagger nonsense'? she wondered. Obviously she was being deceived on some far greater scale than she had previously suspected.

Kent's words about her seemed cruel and unfeeling. But then the memory returned of his demanding lips on hers, and despite all he'd said, she still could not credit that he was totally indifferent to her. The words he spoke and his conduct over the contract were asking her to believe he was wholly selfish and despicable. Yet, her intuition and the treacherous chemistry set off each time he touched her belied these things. The tiredness in the slump of Kent's shoulders and the strain in his voice indicated to Cheryl that his expedition to London had taken a toll he'd been at pains to hide.

Fool, she chastised herself. Why should she care what problems he had?

But the revelation that he was a sick man was like a knife in her heart.

8

Losing Control

Oh lord, Cheryl thought, *why did I have to wake up?* In her dreams she'd been back in London, playing Monopoly with Sue and Mike at the flat. Mike had cornered most of Mayfair and was wearing a top hat — but incongruously still with a favourite T-shirt — and everybody was carefree and laughing.

Now she was back to reality, and a situation which grew increasingly impossible with each discovery she made.

Elsewhere in the house, people were moving around and things were being done. A discreet air-conditioning system hissed pleasant warmth somnolently from vents in the beamed ceiling. Cheryl could hear water running through pipes and the opening and closing of doors. It was time to face the day.

Conquering her reluctance, she tossed aside the rumpled sheets and swung her legs lithely out of bed. She saw the pile of partly unpacked luggage. 'Goodness, you're an untidy brat, Cheryl,' she scolded herself.

Last night she'd wanted only to retreat into bed and let everything else go hang. Now she saw clothing overflowing from her bags in a tumbled mess across the floor. A quick shower, and then she must take hold of herself and do something about it.

When she came back into the bedroom to find something to wear, she found her choices limited. So many of her clothes would need to see an iron before they were presentable. Finally, she settled for a matching short-sleeved knitted top and a blue skirt. She was debating whether to add a cardigan when there was a tentative knock at the door.

'Miss Maitland! Are you awake, Miss Maitland?'

'Come in, Mrs McBride,' she called back. She heard a fumbling, and to her surprise the housekeeper elbowed her way in, carrying a loaded tray.

'Good morning, miss. Cornflakes, scrambled eggs, toast and marmalade, and tea. I thought you might like your breakfast in bed, it being your first morning after all that flying.'

Cheryl was touched. 'You're very kind,' she said falteringly as Mrs McBride set the tray down on the dressing table. 'Thank you very, very much.'

'No trouble at all, my dear,' Mrs McBride said warmly. 'It's only right that we should all be wanting to make you feel welcome.'

'I hope so . . . oh, I do hope so.'

'Now then, what's this? You sound as though you might be doubting what I say.'

Flushing, Cheryl realised Mrs McBride couldn't possibly be aware of what had passed between Kent and herself — that she was here almost under duress, or of what Kent had been discussing last night with Lois Rimmer. She would, at that moment, have dearly loved to confide in any sympathetic ear, especially an older woman's, but she believed she'd no right to unburden herself on Kent's house-keeper.

'I'm sorry, Mrs McBride,' she got out awkwardly. 'I put that badly. I didn't for one moment mean to criticise your hospitality.'

Mrs McBride looked at her search-ingly. 'What did you mean, then?' she challenged.

Cheryl shrugged helplessly. 'You must think I'm very foolish,' she said, deciding she would have to tell at least part of the truth to extricate herself from this ticklish spot. 'But I've got horrible doubts about whether I'll be able to fit in here. Perhaps I didn't think enough about it much earlier . . . ' *Before I was trapped*, she wanted to say. 'Being on an island makes life so . . . confined, doesn't it?'

Mrs McBride beamed. 'Oh, but that won't matter where you're concerned. You're an artist, and I've heard the master already say as how he thinks you're a rather special one, too. And that will make all the difference. It won't be a bit like when Catherine was here. Catherine the Great, we used to call her.'

Cheryl frowned in bewilderment. 'Catherine the — ' she began blankly, but then another voice cut in and she felt her whole body stiffen involuntarily, as though a rasp had been drawn across exposed, receptive nerves.

'Mrs McBride would be referring to my ex-wife Catherine,' said Kent Gordon from the doorway, and he laughed ruefully.

'Hah! I'm afraid she considered herself rather above cartoons, and just about everything else where Cabin Island was concerned, it turned out.' Mrs McBride's hand flew to her mouth. 'Oh dear, Mr Gordon! I do hope you won't think I was speaking out of turn, but Miss Maitland here seemed so dejected, poor thing.'

Kent waved dismissively. 'No matter, Moira, and forgive my intrusion. But I do think Cheryl's position is very different from Catherine's. I trust she has got at least that part absolutely clear.'

His red-rimmed eyes raked Cheryl purposefully from head to foot. His words seemed to her like yet another dig. It was her turn to feel embarrassed. She felt hot and flustered. Why did Kent have to talk like this? It seemed impossible that he was the man who drew the Bubbles strips, which were always full of fun and good humour. Deep down, she felt he was a good and caring person; not that kind of horrible alpha-male who had to strike sparks off independent young women, even the ones they fancied.

Having to bear the brunt of what seemed like oblique criticism in front of the kindly housekeeper was humiliating.

'Mrs McBride had very thoughtfully brought me some breakfast,' she said clumsily, but with the desperate hope of changing the direction of the awkward conversation.

'Good! Enjoy it, won't you? Then perhaps I could show you my studio and we could start to think about some work. I reckon the sooner we get stuck into it, the sooner you'll get over your blues and settle down in the new surroundings.'

Suspecting his sincerity, Cheryl forgot Mrs McBride and hit back. 'You have pat solutions for everything, don't you? But you don't really appreciate how I feel at all.'

'Work is a marvellous panacea, Cheryl.' He paused as though a bitter thought had struck him. 'That is, if one's able to do it, of course,' he added.

Cheryl noticed again the dark rings under his bloodshot eyes and, with a stab of conscience for her reaction to his advice, wondered if his plan was wise. But she said, 'I'll be ready as soon as I've had breakfast. What time will suit you?'

'Nine will be fine. The studio light isn't at its best before then.' He gave them a forced smile and left.

Cheryl felt the tension ebb instantly and said involuntarily, 'He's not very well, is he?'

Mrs McBride chose her words more cautiously now. 'Now don't you worry yourself about Mr Gordon. I'm sure his underlying stamina will see him through. What you can do is help as much as you're able with his work. It's the most important thing for all of us here. But none of us can draw. So it's up to you, my dear. Right now, you're the most important person on this island.'

Cheryl bit her tongue to stop herself blurting, 'That's ridiculous!' More than ever, she believed she was hearing only half the story behind her presence. She was certain Mrs McBride's parting words were more than an attempt to boost her flagging spirits.

She went to the studio at nine, her stomach a knot of nervous expectation, yet determined to teach Kent she was no pawn in his unknown game but a person with a mind and emotions of her own.

Kent was already there, in an open-necked blue cotton print shirt and white cotton drill casual trousers. He was at one of three drawing boards, ruling up sheets of Bristol board into panels with a blue pencil and metal T-square. 'Top marks for lesson one!' he said, looking at his watch.

'But I haven't done anything yet.' Cheryl was momentarily taken aback. Was he already on some devious tack to emphasise his supposed authority?

'You're here on time. You'd be surprised how many people think a successful cartoonist spends the day dreaming and doodling, and then occasionally dashes off a comic master-piece in ten minutes.'

'Oh, for heaven's sake!' Cheryl exploded. 'I'm not that green.'

His jaw set. 'No, of course not, but I can't stress too much how vital it is for us to stick to a strict routine. Without a disciplined approach, everything will fall apart.'

'Spare me the lecture,' Cheryl said. 'I'm aware you haven't brought me here for fun and games.'

Kent sighed. 'Whatever that means, I don't want to know,' he said in a dangerously quiet voice. Then he plunged straight into a quick rundown of his working methods. His normal week would begin with developing ideas for five strips for daily newspapers. 'We don't sit waiting for inspiration. We draw up our ideas in pencil. I favour fairly soft leads, but not too smeary, because they're the easiest to erase.'

Cheryl listened in dutiful silence. Tuesdays and Wednesday mornings were for completing the initial layout of the strips by inking in the outlines and doing the balloon lettering. Wednesday afternoons and Thursdays saw the erasing of the pencil marks, filling in areas of solid black, 'feathering' the shadows and wrinkles, laying on half-tones — using sheets of pre-printed dot patterns with an adhesive backing — and doing the inevitable corrections, touching up with white Snopake paint.

'Phew!' Cheryl said. 'And that leaves Fridays.'

'When we work on the three-deck cartoons the Americans use in colour in their Sunday papers.'

In honesty, Cheryl thought it sounded very dedicated and daunting. Professionally, the challenge left her hovering somewhere between exhilaration and despondency. But she said, 'And this slavish regime is to last for two captive years.'

'For me it'll be a lifetime sentence if I can manage it, and I'll be glad if I can,' Kent replied. 'The work means that much to me. I feel sorry for you if you can't regard your own talents in the same light.'

'Put down again!' Cheryl retorted glibly, but her heart wasn't really in the repartee and her lip quivered. Darn it, how did the man aim his shafts so unerringly? Her own cartooning did comprise a huge part of her reason for living. If it didn't, she would never have been here, never have got herself into this tangle.

Her lapse into thoughtful silence gave Kent the opportunity to finish what he'd been saying. 'Of course, I've told you only the interesting part. The business side, like dealing with my agents and the merchandising industry, I leave entirely to Lois. Now . . . let's get you started.'

The studio was equipped with everything Cheryl had ever wanted. Once Kent had put her to work inking in pencils he had prepared earlier, her gloom soon lifted and she became engrossed in the work.

For about an hour he left her to her own devices, then he came and stood at her shoulder, making her feel clumsy and self-conscious. 'Jolly good,' he murmured approvingly. 'But heavy up these lines in the foreground, will you? And all the ones on the lower side of objects.'

He was right, of course. It was impossible for her to resent or reject his comment, no matter how much she might have liked to retaliate. But she had already drawn in her breath automatically, as though about to say something.

He frowned. 'Don't bother to contradict me,' he advised tightly. 'You'll be wasting your time. Just do it and you'll see I'm right.'

Cheryl flushed a little. 'I wasn't going to say anything,' she said.

'Hmm! You were thinking about it, though.'

His perception was infuriating and the mild rebuke hurt. Though he seemed determined to keep her at a metaphorical arm's length as a person, and made not the slightest effort at small talk, he understood her well. Too well, she thought with chagrin. But he was an expert tutor.

Cheryl quickly realised that the experience and techniques she would pick up under his guidance couldn't be matched any other way.

Kent, too, seemed more relaxed and less strained as the day wore on. 'You know, it fascinates me how well you know my characters and my style,' he admitted.

'I love the Bubbles strip. I've been using your drawings as swipes since I was at school,' she said honestly.

'But you've learned from using them. For many people who lack creative skills, swipes can be crippling, destroying what talent they have. In your case they've obviously been a crutch you've long since thrown away.'

His praise gave Cheryl an absurd surge of pleasure. It brought her up with a start. She wanted to kick herself for such weakness. He wasn't going to get round her that way! She wasn't here for artistic fulfilment, but to meet a contractual obligation he'd cunningly manoeuvred her into for reasons he still hadn't divulged. 'Don't feel you have to feed me crumbs of approval. I can work just as well without them,' she said ungraciously.

He let his tired eyes drift over her mutinous face. 'Oh good.'

She couldn't tell whether the weariness in his voice meant his verdict was genuine or sarcastic, so she kept quiet.

'It's reassuring to know I've such an accommodating pupil. You'd prefer me to tell you only about the things you do wrong then, is that right?'

It wasn't what she'd prefer at all. But again she said otherwise. 'I don't give a fig what you do! And I've come here to work as an assistant, not to be a pupil.'

'Pity, that,' he murmured. 'There's so much you could easily learn. But I'll go along with you as far as possible. However, when you need to be put on the right lines, I'll not hesitate to exercise my legitimate control over your activities.'

'Exercise control?' The nerve of the man!

'Yes, Cheryl,' he said scathingly. 'That's what I'm paying for — and paying very well, too.'

To her ears he made it sound as though she were a total puppet, but she held her tongue. Strictly speaking, she was his employee, and obliged to follow his reasonable requests on the conduct of her work. There could be no arguing about that.

Nursing her grievances, and trying to justify them, she fell silent and tried to concentrate on her drawing, following his sound directions to heavy up the lines he'd indicated earlier.

She cursed herself upon finding that though from a strictly creative viewpoint the work she was doing was not her own, it was marvellously satisfying. True artistry it might not be, but she could gain comfort from knowing she was a skilled technician mastering the rudiments of her trade.

The small disasters during that first exhilarating work session were all Kent's. Despite his declared command of the situation, he was prone to silly blunders that suggested he might be the stranger in the studio. He knocked over a bottle of Snopake, then he couldn't find a can of rubber cement, which Cheryl could see in plain view to one side of his drawing board. And when Cheryl shifted the taboret beside her table, he managed to knock into it, sending brushes and pens flying. Had she rattled him after all with her bid to assert herself?

'Are — are you all right?' Cheryl asked as he fumbled to retrieve the scattered equipment.

'Of course!' he shot back. 'It's just a headache. Tiredness, I expect; a kind of delayed reaction from the flight.' His mouth twisted. 'That and other things.'

Cheryl shifted uncomfortably as his gaze met hers. She could read pain in his bloodshot eyes and the wide, hazy pupils. 'Is there anything I can fetch you?' she asked tentatively. 'Shall I call Mrs McBride?'

He closed his eyes and pressed his

long fingers at spots just below his temples. 'You're asking two questions at once,' he said irritably. 'And the answers are yes and no. I'll come right in a moment. Bring me some eyedrops, please. You'll find them in the top drawer to the left of my drawing table.'

All at once she felt an overwhelming wave of pity for him. She wished she could somehow forget the friction that had seemed to arise unavoidably between them. She was so ridiculously affected that her legs were weak and unsteady as she went across to the drawer to hunt out the eyedrops. But she dared not say anything that would express tender feelings. He would surely rebuff her as he had done in London. And the sting of his words last night with Lois was still fresh and painful. How true that eavesdroppers never heard well of themselves!

Through her own tear-misted eyes, she saw a pharmacist's label on a dropper bottle. 'Pilocarpine nitrate.' The words meant nothing, but this must be what he wanted. She gave them to him and hurried, trembling, back to her work, scared he would see that she was upset, and angry with herself because she was.

But the incident passed and the barrier of reserve between them stayed intact.

* * *

In the subsequent days, Kent grew increasingly enthusiastic about Cheryl's work, and his health appeared to improve. Cheryl suspected that her small successes were contributing to his recovery, affording him some relief from an unspoken and longstanding worry.

But if Kent's mind was more at ease, Cheryl's was the reverse. In spite of her dislike for his dominating approach, she still felt very stirred by him. It was inexplicable; it was infuriating. Contradictions and suspected half-truths abounded in what she had been told. Even Kent's approval of her art had a downside. Being human, she found herself less able to think badly of someone who would openly express admiration for the things she was doing. With the haggard look vanishing from his features, he again became as disturbingly handsome as when she'd first sighted him. His constant presence was an assault on her senses. Womanly longings brought to new and glowing life the spark of attraction he'd so ruthlessly stamped on. Her own imaginings filled her with self-contempt. She didn't want to be aroused by Kent Gordon. Most of all, she didn't want to admit that she yearned to test again the sweetness of his lips plundering hers, his possessive hands upon her, and his lean body crushed against hers in a passionate embrace.

On the fifth day, the constant, unavoidable interaction came almost innocently to a flashpoint. Cheryl was striking out on her own now, initiating some of the drawings, albeit in Kent's style. It was a sign of the thawing of their relationship that Cheryl was able to express her frustrations when the work didn't go exactly right.

'Blast! I'm never going to get this figure looking right.' She reached for an eraser as Kent came up to look over her shoulder.

'Definitely wrong, isn't it?' he said contemplatively.

'But why, Kent?'

'You think I should know?'

'You must, I'm sure you must.'

Kent laughed. 'Sometimes your confidence in me is touching! I don't have answers for everything, you know . . . though I often wish I did.'

Something in his tone made her look at him squarely, determined not to be put off track. 'If that's meant to be another of your subtle reminders that our relationship doesn't extend beyond the studio, please note I was only talking about this drawing.' She tapped emphatically at the Bristol board's matt surface with the end of her pencil.

After a pause, he said as though with regret, 'That's straight talking.'

'So are you going to help me with this?'

'I'm thinking about it. You might also consider that when I told you I wasn't infallible, I might have been talking just about art, too.' He sat down on a stool. Square chin in hand, he studied the drawing from beneath lowered brows. He looked like a statue of a pensive Norse god.

At length, he got to his feet with a rush. 'Yes . . . I think I see it!'

To Cheryl's astonishment, he whipped her work off the drawing board, scattering drawing pins in his haste, and seized her by the hand.

'Where are we going?' she gasped.

'It's a question of anatomy, and we'll need a mirror. It's the only way I can show you.'

Pulling her behind him, he rushed out of the studio and into the wing of the house that contained the bedrooms. Thrusting open the first door, he stormed in.

Cheryl knew he was dragging her into his own bedroom, and she went hot, but he was oblivious to her discomfort. He slapped her drawing end down on the floor against a door-length mirror. 'You'll see — it's perspective and a whole lot more,' he said excitedly.

Wide-eyed, Cheryl took in but tried to ignore her surroundings. A big double bed took up much of the space, its broad expanse beneath a loose-weave cotton spread that looked Indian in design and manufacture. Neutral tones and stained wood gave the room a distinctly masculine ambience, heightened by a lingering trace of spicy cologne.

But Kent's complete engrossment in his argument helped allay the alarm that gripped her. 'You must have realised, like everyone else, that cartoonists don't use proper anatomy.

Heads, bodies, and limbs are rarely shown in correct proportions, are they?'

Cheryl nodded dumbly, trying to keep her eyes solely on her drawing.

Exultantly, he plunged on. 'But it's simply not true to think the successful ones ignore *Gray's Anatomy*. They can exaggerate anatomy for humorous effect, but they can't ignore it. The biggest mistake you can make is to try to create your own proportions before you know the correct proportions inside out.'

'Lesson for an amateur,' Cheryl murmured quietly.

'But maybe you've never tackled it the best way before. Here — ' His hand closed on hers again. ' — come and stand in front of the mirror and reach towards it.'

'L-like this?' she faltered self-consciously.

He grimaced. 'No, no! You look like a wooden doll. Loosen up . . . '

In the mirror she saw his hand moving towards the back of her head.

Her breath seemed to stop in the split second before she felt his fingers touch the nape of her neck, light as a caress. By huge force of will she forced herself to unwind sufficiently to move her head to the more natural angle he wanted.

'There! Now do you see what's wrong with your drawing? You've got the proportions of the hand wrong in relation to the face and body behind.'

Cheryl saw perfectly. But she was quite unable to speak, for as though unintentionally, Kent's hand was now sliding slowly between her shoulder blades, over the strap of her bra, and down her spine to the small of her back. His warm breath stirred strands of hair behind her ear as he spoke. She felt the blood rush madly through her veins, and saw the reflection of the colour burning in her cheeks. Suddenly Kent's eyes met hers in the mirror and she stared back at him tremulously, trying to read the odd expression that appeared in their grey-green depths.

'Cheryl . . . ' he breathed wonderingly, his mood transformed.

Something told her she should move away — and quickly. The voice of reason, perhaps. But it was too late for that. Frozen to the spot, she felt the last vestiges of antagonism towards him melting in a surge of longing such as she'd never experienced before. Folly though it was, she wanted him to put his arms around her and clasp her to him.

Unerringly, he read her body language.

'Oh, God, Cheryl,' he groaned raggedly. 'This is insanity!'

And he drew her to him, his mouth moving caressingly from her ear, enticingly traversing her cheek to find the parted softness of her lips. Then his kiss became hard and totally demanding with the intensity she knew in the deepest part of her heart that she'd not misread the last time. In her inflamed state, she had no defences to deny him her full and eager response. After so many days pent up in his close proximity, the dampened fire burst out of its confines into an all-consuming conflagration of her senses.

She shivered in delight as he slipped the loose neckline of her shirt off one shoulder to brush her skin with his exploring lips. 'So tempting, so irresistible . . . ' he murmured huskily. Then, galvanised by his urgent passion, he swept her effortlessly off her feet and carried her in his strong arms across the room.

Their lips joined again. Cheryl felt drugged by their kisses. The room swirled around her, and her whimper as he lowered her gently down onto the bed couldn't have been even the weakest echo of a protest. He was beside her so quickly, she scarcely knew his lips had left hers. His deft, slender fingers plucked at her shirt buttons, and then the delight of his firm mouth was hot on her neck. She gasped with pleasure.

With a sob, she rolled and her spread

hand left the heat of his heaving back, where his own shirt now clung damply. As if distantly, she heard a clatter as her flailing arm swept across the top of a bedside cabinet. Immediately, she felt something hard and cold become trapped between them.

Not everything she'd knocked down had gone to the floor, it seemed, and Kent was all at once pulling away from her, with what sounded like a stifled curse. Breathlessly, she sat up with a shiver of apprehension, one shaking hand hastily pulling her shirt together.

Kent was holding a small dropper bottle that could have been the twin of the one she'd found for him that first day in his studio drawer. He looked at it, his face ashen. He opened a drawer in the cabinet from where it had tumbled and tossed it in angrily. 'Ye gods!' he said. 'What can I be thinking of?'

Cheryl was devastated, not by the sudden termination of their passion, but by the dawning horror that it had been allowed to start. To enter into an affair with this man, after all he'd said, would be crass stupidity. 'I-I'm sorry,' she whispered as the remorse welled up inside her.

'You're sorry!' he bit out, his hands now clenched into fists. 'I think I need my head examined! I promise you, I won't let it happen again.'

Cheryl jumped to her feet, smoothing her clothes so that he wouldn't notice her trembling hands. 'Of course it won't happen again,' she said, trying to sound brisk. 'I'm here to do work for you and earn money. That's all, isn't it?'

'We both got carried away . . . ' he began lamely.

'Both,' she said, putting a steadying edge into her jerky voice. 'Last time, of course, it was just silly me!'

'Cheryl . . . ' he pleaded.

'Oh, don't worry — I realise I'm of no importance to you beyond my handy talent as an artist's odd-job girl. You made that quite clear before, remember? But I stupidly forgot.'

'Cheryl! I apologise.'

'And being so young and naive, I didn't recognise that, as a male in his prime, you might sometimes have a need for . . . for . . . physical gratification!'

'Cheryl! I apologise,' he repeated. 'You don't know what you're talking about.'

'I do so! I thought you might have some feeling for me after all; might love me. But I was oh-so-wrong.'

'Yes,' he grated, 'I'm afraid we'll have to say you were mistaken. It's the only answer.'

'Total honesty!' she taunted, becoming slightly hysterical.

'I did what you wanted me to, but perhaps I shouldn't have done. Now let that be an end to it,' Kent said.

'But you said you were carried away, too!'

'Please! Stop tormenting yourself. You must get it into your head that I don't love you. We have work to do together, but beyond that there's nothing, do you hear? Nothing!'

Cheryl choked back a sob. 'Kent, I-I can't believe you're . . . indifferent to me.'

'Look, we're going round in circles. I don't want to talk about it anymore. If it helps, tell yourself that it's been part of growing up. You've found out that some men can be aroused without feeling anything more than animal urges, and I must be one of them.'

A shuddering cry escaped Cheryl's lips. 'That's a revolting thing to say. If you really believe it, then you've not only turned your back on civilisation — you've become uncivilised! To think I let you touch me! I'm going to my room.'

'An excellent idea. The sooner this interlude is concluded and forgotten, the better it will be for everybody.'

With that, Cheryl fled, not pausing till she had flung her door shut and locked it. She heaved a sigh of relief that she'd not bumped into the kindly Mrs McBride or the sharp-eyed Lois

Rimmer. They would have been sure to have noticed her distress and asked if everything was all right. Breaking down in front of them would have been hateful.

Now, slumped across the bed in the privacy of her luxurious room, she could let flow the torrent of tears she'd held back so painfully. Things had come to a catastrophic head so rapidly. Could she endure two years of this heart-rending captivity?

9

The Ex-Mrs Gordon

Cheryl was a victim twice over. She'd been drawn into a web of deception and self-deception out of which she now no longer had the power to extricate herself. Nor had she the will.

She'd fallen prey to her own imprudence. The thought of revolting against Kent's tyranny by walking out wasn't considered. Hadn't she helped to spin the web herself? Besides, making a grand exit off a privately owned island wasn't a feasible option.

A calm akin to resignation followed the tearful release of her emotions. The sickening sense of horror which had caused her to shudder and flee in loathing from Kent she washed out of her mind as deliberately as she washed the tracks of the tears from her face.

Then she went and sat quietly by the window, watching a rising wind whirl leaves around the patio and disturb the even play of the fountain.

Carefully she assembled the facts, as though sketching out the rough outline for an important drawing. She didn't want to be in this picture, but she had no choice. The background was Cabin Island, and she couldn't change that either. And, of course, the other main figure in the drawing was Kent Gordon. But his outline was becoming increasingly difficult to capture. It was crippled and twisted by ambiguities. Should he be drawn with a smile or a frown? As a hero or villain?

Whatever, he would regretfully have to be put in the picture at a distance from herself. But she would dare to light the scene with a ray of hope. And if there had to be a cloud casting a shadow, it would be the fact that, although nothing had been said about it to her, Kent's health was unstable. In what way was he ill? she wondered.

Here lay the focal point. If she could only find its correct place, it would make every other part of the composition fall into a natural order.

She clenched her fists till the nails hurt her palms. Kent had to be telling a lie when he said she was of no account to him. She didn't believe he felt nothing towards her except a crude lust. For a start, it didn't fit in with his genuine, glowing appreciation of her work. Nor would pride let her accept that an intelligent man might think he could behave as though their mutual passion had no substance, no sincerity.

As much as the hurtful things Kent had said, Cheryl also regretted the taunts she'd thrown at him. It had been a mistake to accuse him of using her merely for physical gratification — she cringed as she recalled the hasty jibe — and a mistake to say she was wrong in assuming he might be in love with her. All that had done was give him his cue to push the same line.

The first priority now must be to

control the damage done. The second — when and if things could be got back on a more or less even keel — must be to find out what made Kent act the way he did.

A tentative tapping at the door broke into her thoughts. 'Who is it?' she called, her voice still slightly wobbly.

'Only me, Miss Maitland,' called Mrs McBride.

With thumping heart, Cheryl swiftly crossed the room to release the lock and open the door. Mrs McBride beamed at her benevolently. 'It's three o'clock and I thought you and Mr Kent might like a cup of tea. I expected to find you in the studio.'

'I — I was resting.'

'Oh, dear, he said you were feeling a bit under the weather.'

'He did, did he?'

Mrs McBride looked flustered. 'Well, maybe he didn't say it actually, but it was what he gave me to understand.'

Cheryl smiled kindly. 'You're very tactful and loyal, Mrs McBride. But the truth of the matter is we've — we've had a slight disagreement.'

Suddenly the hypocrisy of what she was saying struck her. She couldn't tell lies to a face that looked on her so attentively and sympathetically. 'No,' she went on in a firmer voice. 'The truth is, we've had a blazing row. Did Kent tell you that?'

'Oh, you poor child!' Mrs McBride breathed. 'Here, sit yourself down and I'll bring in that tea. I've got the things right here by the door.'

Cheryl didn't share Mrs McBride's total faith in the healing powers of a cuppa, but she knew it might be recuperative. In the whole house, Mrs McBride's was the only shoulder she could think of to lean on. 'Yes, some tea would be nice,' she said gratefully.

'Here we are, then. Now you tell me what's the bother.'

Cheryl couldn't tell her it was none of anyone's business. Nor could she tell her what had happened in Kent's bedroom. 'I really don't know how to begin . . . ' she said hesitantly. 'I don't want to ask you to tell me anything that would be disloyal, but Kent can behave so strangely.'

'He can, but you mustn't blame yourself. I put it all down to that woman he married. She may be gone, but she's left a horrid mark,' Mrs McBride replied with unexpected vehemence.

Cheryl's eyes widened in surprise and her thoughts rushed wildly along this new line of conjecture. Could the woman Mrs McBride had called 'Catherine the Great' be the explanation for Kent's avowal that love could have no place in his schemes?

'How do you mean, a mark?'

Mrs McBride fiddled with the teapot. 'I shouldn't trouble you with it, dear. Besides, it's a long story.'

'But I want to know. I *must* know.'

The housekeeper studied her curiously. 'I'm not sure that I should . . . '

'You mean, Kent wouldn't be pleased if he knew you were discussing his affairs with me.' Cheryl's lips trembled slightly.

Mrs McBride turned slightly pink. 'No, no — what's common knowledge to the rest of us here can hardly harm him by my telling you. I was thinking of yourself. You might not want to be hurt by old problems, after all.'

'I may already be hurt, as you put it.' Cheryl sighed. 'But whether that's to do with old problems, I don't know enough to say.'

The older woman looked at her again as though with a fresh understanding. 'I'll tell you what I think, then. Miss Catherine Brookfield was a gold-digger. She married our Mr Gordon for his money and his looks. But she'd no appreciation of his talents and his love of his work. Nor could she abide living on Cabin Island. She caused a lot of unpleasantness before she went for the last time. Kent vowed then he'd never let the like happen again. When you arrived, I thought that he might've changed his mind — or that he might one day. And I was glad. Because it isn't natural for a fine man in the prime of his life to be the way he is.'

Cheryl was listening intently. 'And now you think you were wrong — that he hasn't changed his mind?'

It was Mrs McBride's turn to sigh. 'It might be best if you weren't to get . . . involved, mightn't it?'

Cheryl swallowed the lump in her throat. What, she thought, would Mrs McBride say if she knew she was already 'involved'?

'Such a pity,' the housekeeper went on, shaking her head regretfully. 'You sharing his love of cartooning and all, and being so talented, just like him . . . And you can lay it at that Catherine's door for certain!'

'Tell me, then — what did she do?' Cheryl was intrigued. 'How did she make herself so unpleasant?'

'Her smart-set friends from Auckland were the worst. She'd invite them up here on their fancy yachts, and there'd be partying and drinking to all hours.

She could never understand Mr Gordon's insistence on keeping to his work schedule and meeting his deadlines. She was more than friendly with some of the men, too, and to cut it short, that's what led to the final break-up.'

Cheryl sipped tea to cure the dryness in her mouth. 'What happened?'

Mrs McBride heaved another sigh. 'Well, I don't know that it's a proper thing for a nice young lady to hear of . . .'

Cheryl half-smiled. 'I'm afraid in the world today only the smallest of children lead sheltered lives, Mrs McBride.'

The housekeeper briskly stacked the empty cups and saucers on her tray, then sat back and told the story. 'It was in a January, and Catherine had friends here. She wanted Kent to go back to Auckland with them for some sort of summer regatta, but he refused and there was a bit of a scene. Catherine stormed out of the house. When she didn't return and it was getting very late, Kent went looking for her. He found her on the *Tigress*. She'd made free with the drinks cabinet and she was far from sober. She was also sharing a bunk with one of her male friends.'

Cheryl gasped. 'How awful!'

'There was a bit of a brawl and Kent threw the man off his boat. The man made all sorts of threats about laying assault charges, but we never heard anything. When he left in his own boat, though, Catherine went with him. And good riddance, we all said.'

It was a sad story, but no worse than many others Cheryl had heard. Did it explain Kent's antagonism towards her? Had his ill-fated marriage led him to reject the possibility of ever having a meaningful relationship?

Mrs McBride's face was grim. 'Mr Gordon was left a bitter man. Yet he had his work to occupy him, and I had hoped that finding someone who shared his interest would change everything.'

Cheryl felt miserable. 'But now you

fear nothing ever will, and the hurt will go on forever.'

'Just don't let it become a hurt for you, my dear. Nothing could be more unfair. Kent isn't a bad man, but I'm afraid his experience may have made him insensitive to what he might be doing. I often think that when he locked himself away here after the divorce, he also locked up his emotions and threw away the key.'

⋆　⋆　⋆

That night a violent storm shook the island. Whether Cheryl would have slept if the high winds and driving rain had not rattled and lashed the window, she could never know. But she lay awake, tossing and turning, for many hours, mulling over all that had happened and all she'd heard that eventful day.

If what she'd learned from Mrs McBride did have some bearing on Kent's odd behaviour, then perhaps she could cling to some small hope that eventually she could win his trust and then his love. It was nothing she could count on, of course, she warned herself, but it might make her life more bearable if she persevered with the two years stipulated by her contract. Kent's conduct gave her every excuse for breaking the arrangement, but she knew in her heart that she was now doubly resolved to stick with it through thick and thin.

As she grew more and more tired, she began to slip into a hazy half-consciousness where her thoughts were less coherent but increasingly wild. Her wandering mind kept taking her back to the afternoon in Kent's room when he'd carried her to his bed. She relived in her imagination the thrill of being borne in his strong arms and feeling the urgent vitality of his body pressing upon her . . . the sweetness and passion of his kisses.

Eventually her fevered thoughts shocked her into wakefulness and she sat up in bed, embarrassingly aware of her treacherous sensations. What on earth . . . She mustn't allow herself to be possessed by such thoughts! It was madness. Any plan she'd made to play a cool waiting game would be brought to disaster before it had begun. She'd never been so affected by a man. Perhaps it was the change of climate that fuelled these outrageous thoughts. Or was it just that she was getting older, or that she'd cut herself away from the restraints of old friends and familiar situations?

She jumped out of bed and went and sat by a small window on the opposite side of her room to the patio. Through it she could see a patch of starless sky and a small segment of the dark and vast Pacific Ocean. It was no escape — it looked as unreal and murky as her thoughts. A pattern of lights crawled across the scene from left to right almost as though they were on a video screen, but Cheryl knew from when she'd asked previously that they were probably the lights of a container ship on its way down the sea-lane to the port of Auckland. She didn't envy anybody who had to be out there on a night like this, even in a large vessel. The waves pounded the island's shores with a force that reverberated through the foundations of Kent's house as though some huge, erratic machine was installed in the basement.

As she watched from the window, although she wasn't conscious of thinking at all, somewhere deep inside her a resolution was hammered out. She would endure the next two years with all the stoicism she could summon. Perhaps Kent would mellow in that time and his health improve. He'd made it brutally clear he regretted the advances he'd made and that they wouldn't be repeated.

Two years was a long time . . . he might change his mind. But if that miracle didn't happen, she could shift out of his life with the fortune of a hundred thousand pounds, and the knowledge that pride was intact even if happiness had been destroyed.

* * *

A week passed, and Cheryl tried to adapt to the new tenor of her life. No further mention was made of the bedroom incident. But after the first day, and mindful of what she'd heard from Mrs McBride, Cheryl was increasingly uncomfortable, irritated by the long hours of silent work in the studio, most of them with Kent just across the room.

The tension between them was palpable, and she hated it. But it was something neither of them seemed able to help. Their deep mutual awareness — there was no other word for it — gave the air the stifling, electric quality that threatened an eventual storm.

'Are you going to say nothing all day?' Cheryl demanded, anxious to avert the outbreak.

Kent took his eyes briefly off his drawing board to glance at her. His face was a mask. 'There's nothing to say. Your work is still coming along fine, and that's the only consideration.'

'If that's so, you might at least reward me by making the effort to be civil,' she pointed out coolly.

Kent appeared to reconsider his position after that and the atmosphere improved slightly. The fragile truce was restored, and more words passed between them, yet with reserve.

Despite the coolness, Cheryl found Kent, with the exception of Mrs McBride, the easiest person to deal with on the island. Dean McBride was perpetually engrossed in the practicalities of life and inclined to be uncommunicative. Lois Rimmer could be sharp-tongued, and, though she displayed no resentment of her as a person, Cheryl suspected she continued to find her presence on the island a matter for regret.

The sessions of instruction with Kent

became exhilarating again, and it showed in the progress Cheryl made. She worked desperately hard, anxious to demonstrate that their bitter quarrel had no influence on her art. Shared talent and enthusiasm for the work soon created a bond nothing could deny.

'Lois is going across to the mainland today, so we'd better get the finished art together,' Kent announced one morning.

'But it's only Wednesday. I thought we had till Thursday,' Cheryl protested mildly. On Thursdays Lois, who had complete control over the clerical side of the operation, would go into town and organise the scanning and sending of images of Kent's work for distribution to various overseas representatives of the Amalgamated Features Syndicate.

'Apparently Dean's discovered a problem with the radio gear on the *Tigress*,' Kent explained. 'He wants to pull it all out and take it to the service agents. Something in the guarantee gives him the idea they may need to send it down to Auckland, so the sooner the better. Here, I'll give you a hand.' He found some panels that needed spotting. 'Tidy these up with the Snopake, will you, please? I can sort out the rest.'

While Cheryl whitened out the minor inking errors, Kent assembled the other pieces of board on a sheet of brown paper, ready for Lois to wrap and pack in a large black carry-case. When the secretary came in a few minutes later, Cheryl was just adding her corrected cartoons to the small pile. She returned to her drawing board straight away, leaving the packing to Lois.

Then a puzzled exclamation called Cheryl's attention back. 'Hey, Kent!' Lois said. 'There's one too many here. Is one of them part of next week's set?'

'Can't be . . . ' he murmured, going over to her.

Lois spread the pieces out around

her. 'There — apart from the three-decker, you've done seven.'

Suddenly Kent chuckled appreciatively. 'Well, I must say it took even me a moment, but I can see what's happened now. In my hurry, I've bundled up one of Cheryl's practice pieces with my own finished work. Can't you see which one it is, Lois?'

Lois reddened. 'No, I can't, and I don't share your mirth!'

Cheryl, too, felt her colour heighten, but not from anger. Only Kent was unruffled. 'Ah, but at least you must be glad of the proof that my plan is going to be workable,' he told Lois.

She was not placated. 'Proof, nothing! What's one piece? No doubt it was produced with a lot of input from yourself right at the artist's elbow.'

Cheryl felt goaded to reply, but bit her lip as Kent leapt to her defence. 'On the contrary, no help from me at all,' he said gloatingly.

Lois tutted fiercely. 'But I'm sure you would have been at hand to offer advice if it hadn't worked. A consistent, totally independent effort might be a different matter.'

Kent stood his ground. 'Cheryl's making excellent progress. I've every faith in what I'm doing.'

But Lois wasn't backing down either. 'I'll tell you bluntly, Kent, I believe it would be better if the whole madcap scheme was dropped immediately,' she said earnestly. 'You're frittering away your time and energy when you can least afford to. Meanwhile, the stress levels around here have soared sky-high, which was the very thing this was supposed to have avoided.'

'What do you suggest then?' Kent returned.

'Exactly what I've always said.'

'But the situation has changed now. We can't go back.'

'Of course we can. Cheryl should be sent home to England immediately — today! Both of you would be a lot happier. Then you can get on calmly and at full speed with what's got to be done before it's too late.'

'Sorry, Lois, I disagree with you,' Kent insisted. 'And I think this little test — ' He gestured at the seven cartoons. ' — proves I'm right. Even you were deceived.'

'Oh . . . so you're confessing it was a deliberate trap, are you?'

Cheryl gulped and tried to hide her head in her work. But Kent had a ready denial for Lois. 'No, I'm not. It was purely accidental, I assure you. But it illustrates the point very neatly, I feel. Anyway, Dean's already gone down to the *Tigress*. Let's get these packed and you can be on your way.'

Lois glared and opened her mouth as though to say more, but then she thought better of it. Kent swiftly lifted away one of the cartoons and she did as he suggested.

'Phew!' he said as she swept out. 'Lois can be very persistent, I'm afraid.'

Cheryl drew a steadying breath. 'It was very embarrassing, and I'd still like to know why everybody has to be so cryptic. What exactly is . . . '

Suddenly she caught sight of the piece of art that Kent had tucked under his arm. 'Kent! You've picked out the wrong one. That's one of yours. Quick — I'll call Lois back!'

But Kent caught her by the wrist as she moved towards the door. Whether it was the firm grasp of his strong fingers or what he said, an electric tingle ran through her body. 'Don't bother, Cheryl. I know exactly which cartoon I held back.'

She stared at him in blank astonishment. 'You do?'

'Of course,' he said with a laugh. 'If it's good enough to fool Lois, it'll fool anybody.'

Cheryl's conscience pricked as she was abruptly struck by the imminence and enormity of this deception. 'Do you think that's a good idea? As Lois says, it's hard to see anything funny about it.'

'I'm not so much amused as joyful, Cheryl. This, after all, is what I've been working towards, and the goal's in sight before I'd dared to hope. As a bonus, it means I've another cartoon to add to my reserve.'

''Joyful'!' Cheryl couldn't hide the scorn in her voice. 'Well, there's no joy in it for me. The only pleasure is in knowing that I've done a competent job. Beyond that, I'm simply hurt.' She knew she was moving onto dangerous ground, but it was impossible to keep bottling up her thoughts and feelings.

The smile faded from Kent's face. 'Why are you hurt, Cheryl?'

'Because I'm sick of knowing only half of what's going on — maybe less! Why do you need to trick people? To pay me good money to help you do it? Tell me the truth!'

Kent looked at her stonily. 'No, I can't do that,' he said, almost as though talking to himself. 'It's still too soon, and it'll affect you, I know it will. You need more confidence yet. And to be detached, totally detached. Any other way, you won't have the ability or the strength to see it through.'

'Kent! You're still talking in riddles,' Cheryl protested. 'I don't want to be detached, if that's what you call it.'

'Exactly. We've proved that before. And that's why I can say no more.'

Cheryl simmered with impotent exasperation. She simply had to bring this to a head. 'Lois could be right. Perhaps I should pack my bags and pull out of this whole arrangement. To hell with the contract! Just give me a ticket back home. I'll forfeit the money. I won't be able to sell cartoons. I'll have no job and nowhere to live. But I might have some peace of mind.'

Kent was goaded to a fury. Cheryl was alarmed by the vehemence of his reaction. 'Cheryl, stop it, will you!' he flared. It was as almost as though he was scared of her leaving, which paradoxically gave her reassurance.

'Tell me what's really wrong, Kent. Some dark secret is being kept from me, isn't it?'

'No! No!' His face darkened, confirming her suspicion.

She drew back, white-faced, and with a sharp intake of breath through trembling lips; yet her heart filled with new strength and resolve.

Kent closed his eyes and clasped a hand to his brow. 'Sorry,' he muttered harshly. 'I didn't mean to shout. But you mustn't interrogate and threaten me like this. I thought we'd got it all sorted out between us. Believe me, your work here really is vital. Just give it one more go, will you?' He moved back across the room to his drawing table, stumbling into a chair on his way.

Cheryl was stunned by his swift shift from anger to vulnerability. 'All right,' she replied inadequately after a moment's obstinate silence. 'But I think I should talk to Lois when she gets back. It needs to be made absolutely clear that I had nothing to do with what looked like an attempt to deceive her.'

She saw Kent's mouth tighten into a hard line. 'I can take care of that. It's not your problem,' he said with roughness in his voice as if he were in pain.

Cheryl had no real wish to confront Lois over the extra drawing, still less to reveal that Kent had continued to dupe her. It would be a touchy conversation. Lois seemed determined to remain unapproachable, if not actively hostile. Sometimes Cheryl had caught Lois's smouldering gaze fixed on her as if to say, 'You wait!'

'Very well then,' she conceded expressionlessly. 'I must admit I don't find Lois easy to talk to. She's very reserved towards me.'

'I'll speak to her about it,' Kent promised.

The coldness in his tone brought home to Cheryl the depth of her loneliness on this tiny island off the coast of a foreign country at the end of the world. She felt like crying. It was a week since she'd last had a letter from Sue. Two years to go! She was already sick of being unbearably alone and unloved. At this moment she wanted someone to lean on, someone to talk to. She wanted strong arms around her. A man's arms.

She couldn't fool herself. Being engaged to Kent in fact rather than fiction was at the heart of her muddled desires. More than anything, she wanted him to trust her and see her as a woman as well as an artist. She slashed at the Bristol board she was trimming to size with her scalpel, angry at herself for being all kinds of fool. Whatever she suspected about his true feelings, Kent had made it devastatingly clear there could be no romantic entanglements — not once but twice.

Would she get over this rejection? Would two years change her mind about him? Or would she spend the rest of her life longing for him? It was a dismal prospect — her island captivity mirrored forever in an inability to forget and to look at another man.

They worked on in virtual silence, stopping only for a short lunch break. Midway through the afternoon, Kent complained of a nauseous headache. 'We're well ahead,' he said tensely. 'I'll finish for the day now and take a rest. There's no point in suffering unnecessarily, and I haven't forgotten I need to talk this evening with Lois.'

Cheryl felt her heart lurch painfully, but she dared not let him off that hook. 'Yes, do rest,' she advised him doggedly. 'I can finish off here and tidy up your table if you like.'

He briefly squeezed her shoulder as he passed her to leave. 'Now don't you overdo it as well, will you?' he said.

Cheryl forced a smile to her lips, though she felt like crying. 'I won't,' she said quietly, not trusting her voice at much more than a whisper.

★   ★   ★

After dinner, Kent sought Lois Rimmer in the small office she used adjacent to the studio. He'd no more appetite for the meeting than he'd been able to summon for the meal he'd just made a

216

half-hearted attempt to eat.

Lois was unpacking the case she'd taken with her to the mainland that day. He tapped on the door and she looked up in surprise. 'Kent! You look awful. Don't you think you should be taking an early night or something?' For once her voice was gentle, matching the desperate concern Kent knew she all too often masked with waspish asperity.

'I can't see that doing any more good than the rest I had this afternoon,' he told her flatly. 'Cheryl wanted me to have a word with you, anyway. She's got some silly idea you might hold her to blame for the mix-up over the extra strip this morning.'

Lois raised her even eyebrows. 'Is that why you're all washed out and off your food? Anxiety over what's upsetting that kid?'

'Bosh! You know what my problem is. Cheryl has a part to play in the solution. I don't want the pair of you to come to loggerheads, that's all.'

Lois shook her head with a faint

smile. 'Very sound and reasonable, I'm sure. You might believe it, too.'

'Dammit, what's that supposed to mean?'

'Maybe you can't read your own mind as well as others can. I told you what I thought this morning. As well as I could with Cheryl there, that is.'

Kent grimaced. 'Oh . . . ? Tell me more now she isn't.'

'OK, I will. First, you can't keep a person like a bird in a cage for two years. Second, despite all your high-minded denials, I think that girl is affecting you. Perhaps she means more to you than you — '

'Rubbish! I want her here to do the work, nothing more.'

Lois sighed. 'Kent, I'm genuinely sorry for you that you can't see it. But I've actually watched the way you look at her; the way you speak to her. Perhaps it did just start with appreciating her talent — though I'm inclined to doubt even that — but whatever you're repressing now is making you doubly sick.' She slapped her hand on the desk. 'Face up to it, Kent, her presence here is not helping you. Do one thing for me, will you?'

'What?'

'Send her packing. Put her right out of your mind before the whole thing ends in disaster.'

'You don't know what you're talking about, Lois,' he replied hotly. 'I can't send her away. She's irreplaceable. I need her in the studio.'

Lois held up a hand to quieten him. 'There's no need to shout, and you mustn't excite yourself — '

Kent's anger boiled over. 'I'll darn well do as I please! And for a start, that means listening to no more of this fantastic nonsense about what's making me ill. I'll see you tomorrow, when I hope you'll be in a more realistic frame of mind!'

Lois made a helpless gesture. 'If you want to delay the inevitable . . . '

'I'm fully aware of my condition and the need to right it, Lois,' he stormed.

'We've taken the best of specialist advice. The medications can control it for months — even years. My non-existent relationship with Cheryl makes no difference.'

'Kent, you're being terribly unreasonable.'

'Stop talking to me like a nurse! I won't stand for it!' He turned and made for the door.

'Kent!' Lois cried. 'Where are you going?'

'Out!' he yelled. He slammed the door behind him.

10

Peril on a Stormy Sea

Cheryl put aside her book. Above the soothing drone of the easy-listening music from her bedside radio, she could hear voices raised in anger. Kent and Lois were arguing! The suspicion she might be the cause of it filled her with guilty dread. She went cold and her heart thumped. She turned off the radio and swiftly crossed the pale yellow carpet to her door, which she eased ajar.

She couldn't make out what was being said, except for the odd word and her name. Then a door slammed. Cheryl slipped out of her room and cautiously went down the passage towards the front of the house.

Kent was heading for the main entrance, glaring sightlessly ahead of him, looking neither to the left nor the right. A cry rose involuntarily to Cheryl's lips, but she stifled it before it was uttered. Kent was going out, presumably to be alone to walk off his anger. She'd no business to intervene, had she?

Half-reluctantly, she retraced her steps to her room. Then other fears assailed her. He was tired and unwell. What if he slipped or stumbled on one of the island's rocky paths? And she wanted to know what part she'd played in precipitating this latest crisis. Perhaps when he'd cooled down and they were away from the house, he'd confide in her or at least reassure her.

She felt a wave of sorrow surge through her. Oh, what an awful mess it was all turning out to be! On impulse, she pulled on a thick zip-fronted jacket and made her way back to the front door.

A fresh breeze whipped at her loose hair, and she narrowed her eyes as she stood on the porch. The sun was already below the horizon, the light poor and deceptive with evening shadows. She caught sight of Kent striding purposefully down the track that led to the shore and the wharf. Then he was lost among the outlines of the jumbled rocks and gnarled pohutukawa trees that lined the path.

She hesitated only momentarily before dashing in pursuit. She didn't know what she would say when she caught up with him, but it was suddenly a most vital thing that she shouldn't lose him in the approaching darkness.

Cheryl didn't spot Kent again until the slap and wash of the waves on the beach was loud in her ears. He was still walking briskly, although he'd now reached that part of the track which merged with the sands of the beach, making the going heavier. Again she was on the point of calling out, and again she changed her mind.

Kent swung off the track, still not looking back, and oblivious to his follower. He seemed to be plunging onward as though driven blindly by a compulsion that demanded flight from the seat of his problems.

Suddenly, as he swung on to the decking of the wharf, Cheryl realised where he was headed. To the *Tigress*! The minute she saw his intention, she broke into a run, but faster progress wasn't easy. Loose pebbles and exposed tree roots made haste hazardous in the semi-darkness, although she was naturally a light-footed, agile person.

By the time she'd reached the wharf herself, Kent was already aboard the cruiser. A mighty roar split the air as the *Tigress*'s engines were fired into life. Black-backed gulls wheeled over Cheryl's head, shrieking protest.

'Kent!' she yelled as she pounded over the planks. But her voice was lost in the tumult of sound. The boat's twin titanium propellers were churning the water at her stern into boiling froth. Beneath Cheryl's feet, the wharf shuddered and vibrated in the maelstrom.

Kent was still totally unaware he'd been pursued. He stood stony-faced at the *Tigress*'s controls, as though absorbing the boat's brute power into his own body. Was he truly in command, or was the boat? Cheryl could scarcely tell.

She made another snap decision unconsciously, putting her own life on the line. As the *Tigress* took up the drive of her powerful engines and began to edge away, she leapt, landing in the stern of the boat in a slithering sprawl, and clinging for dear life to a deck rail. By the time she'd caught her breath, the *Tigress*, like a torpedo let off, was skimming across the dark swell of the ocean, with Cabin Island a shrinking hump at the centre of its foaming, ever-widening wake.

The swift passage of the boat had whipped the evening breeze into a cutting blast. Cheryl staggered as she strove to reach the steps that led to the cockpit. 'Kent,' she gasped foolishly as she flopped into the cover of the transparent canopy, 'what are you doing?'

He in turn was amazed to see her. He gaped, chalk-white, as though he were seeing a ghost. 'Good God!' he exclaimed when he'd gathered his wits. 'How did you get here?'

'I — I followed you,' she stammered. 'I was just in time to jump aboard as you pulled away.'

'But what the hell for?' he demanded angrily.

She was still taking her breaths in deep gulps. 'Because I was worried . . . didn't know what you were doing.'

'I'm tasting freedom! Escaping from the encumbrances. Just me, the boat, the sea and the sky. Leastways, that's how I wanted it to be. But now *you're* here!' He flung the words at her like splinters off a block of ice.

'Well, too bad,' Cheryl forced herself to riposte through chattering teeth. 'I acted without thinking. But you needn't let it worry you — I won't get in the way.' In truth, she felt half-paralysed with fear. She licked her dry, salty lips. The *Tigress* was rocketing along at what struck her as an uncontrollable speed. A lifted bow smashed through the swell, sending up and enclosing them in huge arcs of white water.

Kent made no effort to slow the boat's wild passage or change course. 'You shouldn't have come,' he protested. 'But I'm not turning back till I feel good and ready.'

Cheryl heaved herself unsteadily into the seat alongside him. 'That's all right. I've said I won't interfere. In fact, I'll probably have to shut my eyes.'

The hard lines around his mouth relaxed a little. 'I'll wake you up when we get back, but it won't be before a couple of hours.'

'I don't th-think I'll sleep.'

'The boat's perfectly safe, you know. Much safer than a car on the road.'

Defensively, she made a point of opening her eyes, straining them to seek out obstacles her reason told her could only be imaginary out here on the limitless expanse of ocean.

Perhaps that was why, not many minutes later, it was Cheryl and not Kent who saw the only sign of onrushing disaster.

At first it was just a lighter speck on the slate-grey swell that stretched emptily ahead of them to a murky horizon. Then it rapidly became a patch, and finally what looked like a sheet of plywood floating just below the water's surface.

Cheryl said nothing. If she had, at the speed they were travelling, it would have been of no use. But really, she thought Kent also would have seen what she saw and taken evasive action.

There was one heart-stopping instant between the time she realised he hadn't, and the *Tigress* hit the submerged hazard. Then her ears were filled with a hideous, ripping, drumming noise.

The boat reared up out of the water, and they were both flung against the screen in front of them. Then the *Tigress* crashed down again, its bow dipping deeply into the water.

It was several moments before Cheryl, stunned, realised that the *Tigress's* engines had stopped and they were spinning idly in their own swirling wash.

'Damn!' Kent cursed. 'Are you still in one piece, Cheryl?'

Clutching her ashen face in shaking hands, she nodded. 'Th-think so . . . What was it?'

Kent scanned the rolling waves around them. 'It's over there. Looks like a shipping container. Lost deck cargo, I imagine. And it's probably done for the *Tigress*!'

Panic choked Cheryl's voice. 'Done for? What do you mean?'

'I mean if we aren't holed, it's a miracle. We've lost the engines for sure. The propeller drives are probably smashed beyond repair.'

Cheryl was horrified. 'What'll happen to us?'

Kent ran the back of a hand across his brow. 'If we don't sink — and we don't appear to be in that danger yet — we'll drift around out here till Lois or the McBrides raise the alarm and someone comes out and finds us.'

'Doesn't anyone know about that lost container?' she asked indignantly.

Kent shook his head. 'If it was lost in coastal waters, it might've been reported and issued as a navigational warning by the Marine Department's search and rescue operation. But if no further sighting is reported, it's removed from bulletins after forty-eight hours.'

'That's terrible!'

Kent shrugged. 'It happens. In international waters there's not even any obligation for masters to report losses. Many don't really bother, except to tell the owners and insurers. In some cases they don't know they've gone till the ship gets into port.'

A simple and amazingly obvious solution struck Cheryl. 'We don't have to wait. We'll radio for help,' she said confidently.

Kent looked rueful. 'The radio's been dismantled for repair, remember? Dean took it over to the mainland just today.'

'Oh, no!' Cheryl wailed.

'So first I check we're not taking on water, then we sit tight.'

A few minutes later he called out, 'Come on below! We're still watertight, thank goodness, and we might as well wait in comfort. We'll be by ourselves at least overnight, so we'd better resign ourselves to it.'

A little of Kent's confidence rubbed off on Cheryl, making her feel less devastated. But she suspected he was putting on a bold front for her sake, partly through fear she would panic.

How long could they survive? Presumably there would be stocks of drinking water and food, though she didn't dare ask yet how much. Moreover, Kent's health, she knew, wasn't as good as he liked to pretend.

'Let's rustle up a meal before the

light fails totally,' he suggested, as though reading her mind. 'There's cooked meats and salads in the fridge-freezer, and plenty of canned stuff in the cupboards in the galley.'

In the event, the tight lump in her chest left her with no appetite, though she thankfully cured the dryness in her mouth with a carton of fruit juice.

Night was gathering fast. While they ate, Cheryl was sure the waves were growing in size. They set the *Tigress* pitching and rolling uncomfortably.

She shuddered. 'The sea's getting rough,' she observed. 'Are you sure we're going to be safe?'

Kent placed a hand on her shoulder in the gloom and squeezed lightly. 'Safer than we'd be in a life raft, which is the only alternative. The *Tigress* will take much worse than this. The one thing that bothers me is how far we might be blown out to sea.'

Cheryl had a scary vision of the huge open wastes of the South Pacific, the only land mere dots of islands and atolls they might never hit. 'Perhaps they'll never find us, Kent,' she whispered.

'Keep cool,' he answered. 'I'll set off a distress flare every hour. Someone might spot us even before morning.'

Cheryl had her doubts. She didn't know for sure, yet thought it unlikely a flare let off out here would be seen from the mainland. And that left the flimsier chance of a passing ship with an alert lookout.

So it looked like they were thrown together with just one another for company for at least the night. How ironic! Under other circumstances, it would be an ideal opportunity for the straight talking Cheryl felt had been avoided. The question kept coming back: why wouldn't Kent confide in her about himself and his illness? She shivered — whether from the coldness that gripped her heart or the growing chill in the air, she didn't know.

'Here, that's keeping too cool,' Kent remarked. 'Why not go and tuck up in the for'ard cabin for the night?'

'You mean sleep in your b-bed?' she asked.

He laughed. 'I can't claim to read your mind, but there'd be nothing to worry about. I plan to stand watch up top, and I did promise you last time that there wouldn't be any funny business between us ever again.'

An angry retort came to her lips, but she stifled it with a swift intake of breath and a clenching of her jaw. 'I wasn't thinking about *that*,' she muttered. But it was at best a half-truth. The thought of sleeping in that big double bed — his bed — had filled her with the strangest of sensations. How could she still feel that way?

'If you want extra blankets, you'll find them in the drawers under the bed,' he said in a matter-of-fact tone. It was a dismissal — a cue for her to go.

'Thank you,' she said simply, trying to assume similar coolness and detachment. She could have said she wasn't cold, wasn't tired, wasn't feeling panicky. But then he would think she was attaching significance to using his bed, whereas of course he needed to be shown it didn't matter a jot.

In the cabin, the rest of the world seemed very remote. Cheryl took off just her bulky jacket and her shoes and wrapped herself in the quilt on top of the bed. She wondered if their absence had already been noted by Lois or the McBrides, and what conclusions they'd reach from it. A disturbing thought struck her — they might think their delay in returning was deliberate; that they were making a night of it!

She felt her heart skip a beat but forced herself to relax. Kent had made it plain to Lois, surely, that he didn't fancy Cheryl and had no intention of letting her interfere with the odd pattern of his life. No, the search would be on — if not now, then at first light for certain . . .

Eventually the rhythm of the rocking boat exercised a soporific effect, and

Cheryl slipped into a drowsy state where she lost track of time.

* * *

She had no idea how long she'd been sleeping when she was jerked abruptly into consciousness. The bed was heaving beneath her, and only a tangle of covers had stopped her slipping to the floor. Somewhere outside the cabin something fell with a sudden clatter against an unceasing and ominous background of creaks and rasps.

Cheryl slid off the bed and staggered towards the door on legs like jelly. 'Kent!' The cry was torn from her throat before she was properly awake.

The door opened before she reached it, swinging back to bounce against its stop. Kent lurched in with a big flashlight in his hand. 'What's wrong? Are you all right?'

'What's going on? Are we sinking?' Cheryl's voice was ragged with anxiety. 'Tell me the truth!'

Kent braced himself against the door frame as the deck rose under his feet. 'We're copping some dirty weather out there. The seas are running pretty wild now, I'm afraid, and there's not much we can do — except pray we don't capsize!'

Cheryl shivered. 'I can't help it,' she confessed, 'but I'm frightened, I really am!'

That moment the *Tigress* pitched violently, and the next thing she knew Kent had dropped the flashlight and they were thrown together into each other's arms. She trembled uncontrollably. He stroked her hair and murmured soothingly in her ear. 'You mustn't be frightened, Cheryl. There's every chance they'll find us. Until then, we've got to keep ourselves fit and composed.'

His breath was warm on her neck, and his shoulder felt solid and strong beneath the roughness of his woollen sweater.

Cheryl felt her strength renewing in his comforting embrace. The flashlight rolled with the sway of the boat, sending its beam careering crazily across the bulkhead behind the bed. 'I'm sorry,' she moaned. 'I can't believe any of this is really happening to me. It's almost as if I've died already and woken up in another world!' She shuddered.

Kent held her from him at arm's length. 'Here, I took a flask of rum with me up top. Have a tot — it'll warm you up and steady your nerves.'

She sank down on the edge of the bed and took the drink from him. It burned her throat and she spluttered. But its warmth quickly spread inside her, unravelling the knot of fear in her stomach.

Across the cabin, the door swung shut with a bang, cutting off the howl of the angry gale outside. Perhaps it was because Cheryl wasn't used to drinking neat spirits, but the atmosphere inside the cabin was suddenly very warm and close. For the moment the whole turbulent world outside could best be forgotten. All that mattered was this isolated bubble of reality that perhaps would never be reunited with it.

She suddenly realised Kent was talking to her. ' . . . so if you're OK now, I'll let you have the place back to yourself.'

Impulsively, Cheryl reached up and clutched his hand. 'No!' she blurted. 'That is — I mean, if there's nothing you can do outside, I'd like you to stay here.'

He sat down beside her and put his face in his hands.

'Cheryl,' he groaned brokenly, 'do you know what you're asking?'

'I think so. And I want you to know it won't matter . . . Please, hold me in your arms again. If we — we get carried away, I shan't mind. If we s-survive, I'll pretend it didn't happen.'

He expelled what sounded like a tortured sigh, then turned and clasped her to him. She melted instantly into his arms as his mouth closed posses- sively over hers, and he gently bore her down across the bed.

For minutes they just clung to one another, their kisses tinged with sweet despair.

The crippled *Tigress* swung them up and down in a rocking motion. Kent's first caresses were full of comfort and tenderness. But as his knowledgeable hands stroked Cheryl's neck and shoulders, excitement quickened her pulse in an arousal of passion. And each rock of their strange cradle sent her heart lurching to her mouth, then back to meet the aching need that grew in the very centre of her being. She shivered, but not from the cold.

'Cheryl,' Kent whispered, 'you don't know how much I've wanted to do this.'

She snuggled against him. The *Tigress* tossed beneath them, and they clung together in an excess of caring and love.

Cheryl was at peace, more at peace than she'd imagined possible in this perilous situation. At last she felt wholly at one with Kent. Now there would be nothing they couldn't share.

It was as though they were sealing a pact.

★   ★   ★

She woke up slowly at first, as though reluctant to leave behind a sweet dream. The insides of her closed eyelids were pinky grey.

Daylight! And the *Tigress* had weathered the storm . . .

She groped for Kent. Her last memory was of curling up next to the warmth of him as he pulled blankets around them and smothered her smiling face with little kisses. But her searching hands told her she was alone between the rumpled sheets. Kent was gone. She opened her eyes then and saw he was not in the cabin either.

Hurriedly, she tossed aside the covers and jumped out of bed to gather her discarded clothing. She caught sight of herself in a wall-length mirror, and nonsensically paused to inspect her reflection. No. Shatteringly changed though she might feel inside, she was undoubtedly still the same person as she'd been before she'd abandoned herself to the comfort and the joy of Kent Gordon's arms. But as she averted her eyes, it struck her the face might look a little flushed. And wasn't there a new vitality in that always slightly too lanky body, a womanly assurance and pride?

It mattered only just a little to her that she was without her own toiletries and make-up. She seldom used more than a light cream powder blush and the faintest of lipsticks, while her hazel eyes, naturally bright and alert, were passable without the aid of mascara or eye shadow.

Almost reluctantly, she pulled on her crumpled clothes to go and seek the man who surely was now truly hers.

He was leaning over the stern of the *Tigress*. Not noticing the dejected slump of his broad shoulders or his moody gaze, Cheryl called out the instant she saw him. 'Kent! The sea's calmed and the sky's clearing. We'll be saved, won't we?' Her delight brought an added lilt to her Northumbrian accent. But when he turned she was shocked to see the inexplicable misery written on his face. 'Kent, what's the matter? We are going to be all right, aren't we?'

'Very likely,' he grated. 'I've been doing some calculations, and I figure we haven't drifted more than twenty miles, which is nothing to a searching chopper or plane. So we'll be rescued, and I'll have to live with my guilt.'

'Kent! What do you mean? You couldn't help what happened to the *Tigress*.' Concern edged Cheryl's voice and darkened her hazel eyes.

'The *Tigress*!' he exclaimed, hoarse with incredulity. 'It's not the blessed boat — it's you!'

'M-me?'

'Oh, Cheryl,' he groaned, 'I must have been out of my mind. I shouldn't have made love to you.'

She was shaken and bewildered. 'But I wanted you to. I let you.'

'And to my deepest shame, I took advantage of you,' he said brokenly. 'Your trust, your eagerness.'

'But why shouldn't you?' A terrible void seemed to be opening up inside her. It sapped her strength and left her trembling and weak. This conversation seemed so eerily like others she'd had with him, but ten times worse.

'Last night was a ghastly mistake,' Kent said harshly. 'I had no right. I can promise you nothing for the future. I can only offer you a miserable apology and the sincere advice that you forget it ever happened.'

The fateful words hung in the damp sea air. Cheryl felt suffocated by them. *Forget it ever happened . . . Nothing for the future*. His cruelty was beyond comprehension. She had no regrets. She had told him as much. Why he should behave like this again, she'd no idea. Her deepest instincts told her his emotions were genuinely stirred by her.

The attraction was something more than just physical, she was convinced.

She was deeply confused and hurt, but determined not to show it. No actress, she couldn't stand there looking as though she didn't mind his rejection while all the time she ached inside. She turned away from him. 'I don't think we should talk about it just now,' she said courageously. 'I'm going back to the cabin. Call me if anything happens, won't you?'

Returning to the master cabin was like descending into the very pit of despair. But she was drained of the strength to confront him; to challenge yet again the wounding ambiguity of his behaviour. It would be the easiest thing in the world to break down; to cry into a pillow. Only her sorely tried spirit saved her.

She made herself a vow: *I'll find out what's at the bottom of all this if it's the last thing I do.*

It was an unreal hour later, long after Cheryl had stripped the rumpled sheets off the bed and folded them in a neat pile. She was combing out the long strands of her hair with a borrowed comb in the cabin's en-suite compartment. The tangles were long gone, but she was continuing the movements mechanically when she heard a new sound above the muffled lap of the waves which swirled around the drifting boat. It began like the drone of a summer bee but grew rapidly to what was unmistakably the sound of an aero engine. She dropped the comb and rushed from the cabin.

Outside, the strong light made it impossible at first to look up into the sky. An even overcast of high cloud made one huge canopy of glaring whiteness. But eventually she saw the small single-engine plane swooping towards them. Its roar filled her ears and a shadow rushed across them as it passed over.

Her dazzled eyes flickered across to

Kent. He was waving to the plane, but his movements seemed slow and heavy. The pilot acknowledged his signal with a waggle of the plane's wings. He circled the scene, swinging away from the white glare of the obscured sun, towards the west and the invisible shores of New Zealand.

Cheryl stared after the plane. 'What a relief!' she sighed to Kent. 'How long will it take them to get someone out to us?'

He turned towards her with reluctance. Lines of strain hardened the set of his strong, handsome face. 'No more than a few hours. That plane looked like a private club job, so maybe Lois has been discreet enough to spare us an official Search and Rescue operation.'

'Is that good?' she asked in innocent puzzlement.

He laughed harshly. 'As good as anything about this mess can be! Whoever comes out to us, I don't need to tell you to be careful what you say. You're my fiancée, remember? But I'm sure no one is likely to question us too closely. They'll probably just use their imaginations.'

Cheryl's cheeks flamed and her mouth twitched. 'I don't — ' she began, then broke off and exclaimed in frustration, 'Oh, what's the use!'

She'd been about to comment that her only reason to disillusion them untruthfully might be Kent's own absurd attitude towards what had happened. But that would at best do no more than set off another round of exchanges. She'd no taste for it. It would be too crude a way to give expression to the true depth of her emotions. After all that had now passed, she'd feel as though she were degrading herself.

Kent's mood of self-reproach and her own feelings of betrayal made their wait more uncomfortable than it could have been. But Cheryl was glad their sea ordeal at least was nearly over. When the dot of an approaching vessel appeared on the horizon, she was numb with weariness, and a pain squeezed her chest like a constricting band. Physically, she was now safe, but mentally and emotionally she felt still adrift on a wild and stormy ocean. How could anything ever be the same again? Outwardly the pattern of their lives would have to be resumed, but subtly it would have been undermined and changed, regardless of Kent's remorseful protestations. Restoring and maintaining the previous working atmosphere would call for a huge forced effort on both sides.

The boat that had come out to them was an ex-navy patrol craft manned by Dean McBride and two other men Cheryl had not seen before but who were presumably based at the mainland harbour used by the *Tigress*. They subjected her to inquisitive looks, but she was left out of things as they arranged a tow. They were very respectful towards Kent, but couldn't disguise their incredulity.

'Shame that you didn't spot the

ruddy container that caused all the damage,' one of the boaties said.

Cheryl found herself saying defensively, 'The obstacle was barely floating. Just under the surface really . . . quite hard to see.'

Kent cut in. 'Oh, let's not get into apologising for my shortcomings.'

The boaties moved away, but one glanced towards Cheryl with what was suspiciously like a leer, and she heard him murmuring something unfair about 'distraction'. She was tempted to make a rejoinder, but what would be the point? People believed what they wanted to believe.

Their rescuers took them back to Cabin Island. Cheryl saw two figures making their way from the hilltop house down to the jetty. Mrs McBride and Lois Rimmer had apparently been watching for their return. A reception committee, she thought, her insides churning. She didn't relish the questions that would be put to them, knowing the answers they'd get would be only part of the story, if not evasions.

The *Tigress*, cast off from the tow, drifted into its mooring. It struck the piles of the jetty with a solid thump. Cheryl's heart jumped into her throat. She could hear the thud of her pulse inside her aching head. Kent came up behind her. Clutching the boat's rail, she forced herself to walk forward. She stepped on to the jetty — and into Mrs McBride's motherly arms.

'My dear, what a dreadful time you must have had. It blew an absolute gale most of the night! You must be worn out.'

Cheryl tried to smile. 'There wasn't much we could do, and I did manage to get some rest,' she assured her.

'But it must have been terribly frightening. We've been sick with worry. I couldn't sleep a wink.'

Lois Rimmer skirted round them to lay a hand on Kent's arm, her eyes sweeping his face searchingly. 'Thank goodness we found you quickly. You are all right, aren't you?' The sharpness in

251

her voice betrayed the depth of her concern.

'We lived, Lois,' he said, 'but it was a complication we could have done without. What we all need most now must be some proper rest, I guess.' His voice was tinged with a bitter resignation, and his face looked like it was carved from granite.

Mrs McBride clapped her plump hands. 'Of course! Let's get up to the house. The chat can wait till later.'

Lois broke in. 'I expect Kent and Cheryl have long tired of talking.' She gave a wry laugh and cast a meaningful look in Cheryl's direction. 'I suppose you know everything about one another now.'

Cheryl felt a wave of heat course through her. Lois's powers of perception could be very unnerving, but her caustic comment could be absolutely right or all wrong, depending on what she meant. And Cheryl didn't feel brave enough to probe the enigma.

Part of the way up to the house,

heavy rain overnight had washed down part of the bank onto the track, covering it with loose fragments of rock. Cheryl and Mrs McBride stepped over the treacherous surface, but Kent, beside Lois a few paces behind them, appeared not to see it. His footing slipped and Lois gave a startled cry. 'Watch out, Kent!'

But it was too late. Kent was normally nimble on his feet, as Cheryl had seen before, but tiredness had taken its toll of his natural agility. He couldn't recover his balance, and to avoid slamming into Lois, he fell to one side, putting out his arm behind him to save himself from a heavy fall. Even so, he tumbled awkwardly.

He grimaced as he landed on his backside on the path. 'Heck,' he said in clipped tones, 'I'm getting terribly clumsy!' He went to lever himself up, but as he put pressure on his spread hand, he winced and crumpled back into a sitting position. He gripped his wrist in his other hand and groaned.

'Blast it! I think I've fractured my wrist!'

Cheryl gasped in horrified exasperation. 'Oh no! Couldn't you see where you were treading?'

Lois glared at her as though the accident was somehow her fault. With cold, cutting resentment she asked, *'Didn't he tell you he's going blind?'*

An overwhelming wave of desolation swept over Cheryl and she went totally numb. She had never felt a shock quite like it in her whole life.

11

Truth at Last

Cheryl stirred cream and sugar into hot black coffee with careful deliberation, glad of something to do that might steady her trembling hands. She felt sick when she thought of the thoroughness with which Kent had kept from her the secret of his failing sight. But above all, she was heart-stricken by the awful tragedy of it. To think that Kent Gordon's brilliant talent hung under such a fatal cloud!

Back at the house, it hadn't taken long to confirm Kent's fear about his wrist. Mrs McBride had strapped it up and put his arm in a sling. He'd prowled up and down the big lounge like a restless animal in a cage.

'We'll have to get you across to town and have an X-ray, you know,' the housekeeper insisted.

'Of course, of course,' he muttered impatiently, 'but it's my work that's the worry. I won't be able to draw with a broken wrist.'

Lois, out of all of them, was coming to terms with the mishap the most readily. Perhaps because she knew so much more than the others, her business-like mind was calculating at top speed how best to win an advantage from the disastrous turn of events. Her mouth twisted in crooked irony. 'Well, if you can't draw, then perhaps you'll have time to be sensible at last. For a start, you can scrap this crazy plan of training a stand-in and contact your eye specialist immediately.'

He slumped into an armchair, his face stony. 'The sclerotomy, of course,' he muttered huskily, almost to himself.

'God knows you've been putting off surgery long enough,' Lois said impatiently.

'If you need an operation, it makes sense to have it right now,' Cheryl put in quietly. Her mind whirled with fears and misgivings.

Kent turned on her savagely and she flinched. 'You know nothing about this, Cheryl. I'm more than ten years younger than most sufferers of my condition. The doctors told me it can be controlled with drugs for years.'

Lois shrugged despairingly. 'And so you let the attacks become more and more frequent as time goes on. More pain — acute and sick-making pain — and all the time your peripheral vision gets slowly worse.'

Cheryl felt driven to back up Lois's sober pleas. 'You're being stupid, Kent!' she cried, heedless of his hurtful dismissal of her sensible suggestion. 'Your money can buy you the best attention here or anywhere in the world.'

'OK, OK, but it's a matter of timing, that's what I was trying to tell Lois. With my plan, even if things went wrong, or if my recovery was pro-longed, you would have been the back-up to tide us over.'

Lois scoffed. 'You know what I think about that. Cheryl's training has never been worth the necessary delay. Your dependence on medication has increased. More than that, you've suffered the inconvenience of recurrent attacks which an operation could have ended.'

Lois's grim report put guilty dismay into Cheryl's heart. Kent had to have the operation! She licked her dry lips. 'Lois is right, Kent. You can't draw with your wrist strapped up. Take her advice if it's at all possible.'

Kent looked at her oddly, as though noticing her sheet-white face for the first time and wishing she wasn't there. His face bore no sign of trepidation or anxiety; just resignation, perhaps. 'It can be set in motion any time, I understand. The private hospital in Auckland would be able to take me at short notice, apparently. That makes it a case of securing the best eye surgeon available.'

Lois said briskly, 'Give me the word and it can be done today.'

Kent studied his wrist, scowled, and flexed his bandage-encumbered fingers. 'All right,' he grumbled at last. 'I know when I'm beaten. Let's get it done.'

Lois sighed with satisfaction. 'Well it's an ill wind, as they say, but maybe it'll have done some good if it halts this enthusiasm for working with Cheryl. I'm sure it's been undermining your health.'

But Kent wasn't admitting anything. 'On one hand, the scheme's been very successful,' he shot back, his words tipped with flint. 'We're several weeks ahead of deadlines, so our worries are less pressing there. When we've had a bit of a rest, I'd like Cheryl to come to the studio and we'll sort out exactly what the position is, Lois. I think you'll be pleasantly surprised when I'm able to tell you.'

Cheryl's muscles went tense and her pulse raced. Would the dramatically changed circumstances bring her own situation to a head, as she dearly wished? Or would Kent continue to keep her at arm's length? She felt doubly distressed: by learning of Kent's condition, and because he hadn't confided in her. Despite the kisses they'd shared and the wealth of opportunity he'd had to explain all, he'd told her only half-truths about his motives for bringing her to the island. And only that morning he'd been determinedly and unsparingly critical about the dizzying relationship that had developed between them.

Cheryl went to her room, her body heavy and sleepy after the tempestuous events of the last sixteen hours. After the luxury of a warm shower, she set the alarm on the clock radio for three o'clock, which would give her four hours' rest before the planned stock-taking with Kent.

In fact, she woke just before two. The house was silent except for the creaks of timbers and roofing steel expanding in the afternoon heat. But from outside, Cheryl could hear the rustle of the shrubs on the patio, the tinkle of the fountain, and the chirping of birds. Even with the curtains closed, the strong daylight invaded the room, making it impossible for her to prolong the siesta.

Her waking thoughts whirled chaotically through her mind. But the sleep had crystallised her myriad concerns to the point where one issue overshadowed all others: Kent's eyesight was under threat. As the enormity of this struck her anew, her heart stopped with a great, dropping thump, then began again with quickened urgency. She felt the beat of it behind her ribs, in her throat, in her head.

It was imperative that Kent's sight should be saved before a thought could be given to the unsatisfactory state of other matters between them. She told herself ruthlessly that her own sorrows had more to do with vanity and wounded pride than much else. A hotness, of shame perhaps, flooded her cheeks, and tears of mortification came to her eyes. But what were these things compared to blindness?

With her priorities fixed in her mind, she went along to the studio several minutes early, to find Kent already there. Papers and artwork were piled unevenly on the floor. Several drawers and cupboards had been left open. Nervously, she stumbled into speech. 'I haven't kept you waiting, have I? You did say after three.'

His swift glance made her feel intensely self-conscious, but his strong face was set and unreadable, like a bronze mask.

'No problem. Now the die's cast, I felt I had to make a start, even if it's been a tad awkward using just my left hand.'

She gulped. 'H-how does it look?'

'Reassuring. There are Bubbles strips in just about finished form to meet commitments for five weeks. That pile there — ' He gestured to a stack of pencilled art. ' — is roughs you could easily complete.' He picked up a bulky folder. 'And here are scripts and ideas in note form if things go really wrong.'

She choked back her true feelings. 'They're not likely to, are they?'

He gave a shrug of resignation. 'I'm not an ophthalmologist, but I do know about my cartoons, and I'd say you're more than proficient to sit in for me as long as necessary.'

Cheryl looked around in sudden confusion. 'It'll be different when you're not here.' She felt a stab of panic. 'We're well ahead of schedule. Perhaps I should come to Auckland with you.'

There was a short silence, and his brows knit together. 'I'm not sure that would be a good idea,' he said flatly. 'What purpose could it serve?'

Cheryl felt a churning of emotions deep inside her, but she knew she had to sound calm and controlled. Was that to deceive herself or just him? She gave what could sound a reasonable explanation. 'Because it might look odd if I didn't.'

'Odd?' he asked tersely.

'Yes. We got engaged, remember? It was in the papers here as well as in London. It wouldn't look right if I stayed away. And someone might notice — a hospital receptionist, a nurse, anybody!'

His mouth twisted. 'Well, I suppose you can't be too careful,' he commented dryly.

'So when you go to Auckland, I'll come, too . . . yes?'

He frowned again. 'Darn it! You're probably right. Yes, you'd better come. But just for a day or two. Then I want you back here, you understand? Lois will be quick to remind us you aren't employed to fuss over me.'

Cheryl took deep, steady breaths to disguise her shaky relief. 'I don't intend to fuss, but it'll be rather important for me to know how your operation goes,' she said without specifying why.

Kent responded with careful deliberation. 'It'll affect the kind of work you'll be doing for the next few weeks, certainly.'

She turned away from him and gave her attention to the artwork on the floor. She hoped he hadn't caught her grimace of pain or the mist of tears that glazed her eyes.

The exchange set the tenor of their dealings for the two days that were to pass before their departure for Auckland. For one thing, Kent spent less time in the studio. 'I find it frustrating being in a work environment and unable to work,' he said.

But it was equally galling for Cheryl, who was able to work. The studied formality that marked their conversation, the care Kent took not to so much as brush against her or touch her hand when he stopped by to give guidance and advice, the aloofness of his manner . . . all were intensely frustrating. She longed for him to relent and hold her in his arms again. Her body remembered the things he wanted them to forget, quickening her heartbeat and opening an aching void of longing deep inside her. Why did he still have this effect when he'd made it so plain she had no place in his personal life?

Even in the solitary darkness of her room, there was no escape. When she slept, she relived their stormy night of passion aboard the crippled *Tigress*. She woke, quivering, to a renewed sense of loss and loneliness. But Kent maintained his reserve to the very last.

There were four of them in the car for the trip down to Auckland. Dean McBride drove and Lois took the front passenger seat. In the back, Cheryl was acutely conscious of the muscular firmness of Kent's thigh scant inches from her own. At times when their bodies shifted to the twists and turns of the car, they were almost touching. But the prolonged proximity made no difference. Throughout, Kent remained blank-faced and distant.

When they reached Auckland, Dean drove directly to a wide tree-lined street on a ridge to the east of the city centre. Here the specialist had consulting rooms in an old converted villa.

Typically, Lois had the timetable organised. 'Dean and I will proceed to the hotel, where I've made our reservations,' she announced. 'We'll return to take Kent on to the hospital after his appointment.'

Cheryl took her courage in both hands and elected to stay at the specialist's. Lois threw her a barbed look. 'Really, Cheryl, there's nothing you can do except read dog-eared magazines in the waiting room. And can't you see that Kent is tired?'

Cheryl took in his pallor and noticed the beads of perspiration on his brow. The wave of compassion that swept through her doubled her determination to stay. 'It's exactly what any real fiancée would do,' she pointed out.

'Oh, for Pete's sake. Now we're here, don't let's start arguing,' Kent said. 'Let her come in with me if she really wants to.'

They had about ten minutes to spare, and a nurse-receptionist showed them into an empty waiting room. 'There really was no need for you to stay,' Kent said stiffly to Cheryl after the young woman had gone.

She shrugged. 'I'm in no hurry to get to the hotel. I expect to be there for a couple of days — until we know how you are.' It was a struggle to sound at ease.

Kent stretched out his long legs as he settled down on the couch beside her. He fixed his stare on the carpet midway between their feet. 'There's no need for that either. Lois will be taking the opportunity to see our art-supplies people and visit the insurance office about the claim for the damage to the *Tigress*. But after that, she and Dean will be driving back north tomorrow. If you'd any sense, you'd go with them. Easier for everyone.'

'Fiddlesticks!' Cheryl blurted. 'It'll be

no harder for me to catch a bus. What's the point of Dean having a hired boat on hand if it isn't to be used as much as necessary? It's just a waste of the rent.'

Kent cursed under his breath. 'You really won't let go, will you?'

'My work schedule won't be clear until we know how the operation's gone,' she argued. 'You've said so yourself. And perhaps I'd like a day or two off in an actual city.' Freed from the constant audience of Lois and Dean, she was at last making an incursion through Kent's barrier of restraint.

When he spoke again, his voice was sharp. 'What an insistent person you are! A sightless man would find you the very devil!'

His words forced a shiver of dread through her. Why couldn't he see she was so helpless to alter her feelings? 'You mustn't say things like that.'

'And you shouldn't imply I begrudge you time off,' he responded in a lame attempt to shift the conversation back to less perilous ground.

'Please forget I said anything about a day or two in the city.'

His expression froze again. 'I will. It's you who needs to learn how to forget. Perhaps I should release you from your contract now. After all, it looks as though we've achieved enough . . . leeway.' He shook his strapped wrist. 'And this has precipitated things rather.'

'But you've got to have your operation,' Cheryl whispered in confusion.

'Of course,' he said bitterly. 'But there's really no further reason for you to bother yourself about me and my stupid ailments. If the op goes OK, Lois will be able to cope, won't she? The other arrangements can stop as of now.'

Cheryl felt stunned, as though he'd slapped her in the face. He'd told her to forget before, that she'd no place in his future; but now he was telling her everything was best finished between them immediately. Her sense of stifling, helpless panic rose. She was enveloped in a black cloud. Distantly, she heard her own voice mumble piteously; felt her lips moving thickly.

'I'm sure I can wait a little longer. Maybe we can talk about it afterwards . . . '

But Kent wasn't prepared to compromise. 'It's time to make the break, Cheryl Maitland. Go away; go quickly. You've already got too involved. Lois and I have discussed it. Our contract was a bad idea from the word go. Impractical.'

'No — you needed help!'

'Well, I'm through with the help, and you might as well know it. You need to consider your own life and think about getting out of mine! I can't take any more.'

By now the blood was roaring in Cheryl's ears. 'You don't mean this, Kent,' she managed to whisper. Then the room swam around her briefly before she slumped forward, fainting.

★   ★   ★

271

When Cheryl came to, she was sitting in a different chair and the nurse-receptionist was bending over her, offering her a glass of water. 'I'm sorry,' she muttered. 'I couldn't help it. I passed out.' She felt embarrassed by her weakness.

The nurse was sympathetic but brisk. 'Here, take a sip of this, loosen your belt, and undo the top buttons of your shirt.'

Cheryl struggled up. 'I'll be fine in a minute or two. I don't usually do things like that. It must have been the car journey. I'll be just fine . . . '

'Well, you're still chalk-white, my dear, so maybe you'd better take it calmly for a few more moments. And I quite understand. You must be worried sick about your fiancé, car journeys apart.'

She felt her stomach contract in nervous alarm. 'Kent! Where is he?'

'He's through with Dr Petersen right now, so there's no hurry. Take some deep, steadying breaths and get some colour back in those cheeks.'

'He's going to be all right, isn't he?' she said wildly.

The nurse looked at her searchingly, as though assessing how much she should tell. Her eyes fixed momentarily on the impressive engagement ring Cheryl wore. 'If he really does mean to follow Dr Petersen's advice this time, then he has the best possible chance in the world,' she said with professional caution.

'Kent doesn't really talk much about his — his condition,' Cheryl said tentatively.

'I expect he doesn't like to worry you,' the nurse said kindly. 'Putting it simply, his symptoms all arise from a build-up of fluid in the back part of the eyeball, causing a rise in pressure. Kent's case is unusual because of his age; we rarely see cases in people under forty.'

Cheryl drew a trembling breath. 'Are such things cured?' she asked.

'Frequently. Dr Petersen can make

an incision that will allow the fluids to filter out again and lessen that sickening pressure in the eyeball.'

'I see. And what if Kent just continued taking his medication?'

'If that obstinate man of yours keeps on putting off the operation, then the attacks he suffers will grow more and more frequent and his vision will get steadily worse.'

'Are you sure?'

'Not a doubt about it,' the nurse said. 'The pressure will cause damage, especially to the optic nerve fibres.'

Cheryl sighed deeply. 'Thank God he's given in. Oh, I do hope he's not left it too late!'

The anatomical details of Kent's complaint had not helped her feel less queasy. Why did she care so much when he'd no time for her, or even for her help in his work?

Outside, a car was reversing into one of the visitors' parking spaces. The nurse patted Cheryl on the shoulder, her eyes gentle. 'Here are your friends back again. And doctor shouldn't be too long with the patient now.'

The next half-hour went by for Cheryl in a daze. When Kent reappeared, he expressed concern about how she'd fainted, but Cheryl wondered how solicitous he would have been if they weren't under the eagle eye of Dr Petersen's nurse.

'Normal people don't keel over for no reason. Are you sure you're well?' he asked.

'It was the travelling, I expect,' she lied again.

The nurse — bless her — backed her up. 'Now then, Mr Gordon, don't you go taking extra worries on board for no good reason. The doctor wants you fit and ready in that hospital bed tomorrow morning, so he can get stuck in at last to fixing you up.'

Cheryl suffered a sour look from Lois. 'Buck up, Cheryl,' Lois admonished her. 'We don't need another invalid on our hands, do we?'

She didn't trust herself to speak on

the short journey to the hotel, and once there she retreated without delay to her room, truthfully pleading a headache. The others made no attempt to dissuade her.

Alone, and feeling unloved, she lay on the strange bed in a strange city far from anywhere she'd ever called home, shivering in a fever of wretchedness.

★   ★   ★

Next morning they drove to the hospital beneath an unbroken grey sky in a steady rain. Cheryl knew fatalistically, even from her limited experience of the weather in these latitudes, that the rain was likely to persist for hours.

'Well, I shan't be missing much today, shall I?' Kent commented in an attempt to lighten the gloom. 'Lois won't be much company for you, Cheryl, unless you like traipsing round offices. What'll it be — the shops or the museum?'

'I haven't made up my mind,' Cheryl

hedged. 'The main thing will be not to get in anyone's way.'

A quiver of her lips marred the independent ring she'd wanted the words to have, but Kent wasn't, or chose not to be, swayed by that. 'You should give some serious thought to the advice I gave you yesterday,' he stated in level tones.

She quickly swallowed to clear the lump in her throat. 'I'm getting round to it.'

He gave a grim nod. They hurried from the car headed for a short flight of steps to the porch of the hospital. Dean stayed with the car, but Lois went with them and straight to the admissions desk inside the foyer.

She came back to them accompanied by a nurse. 'Sister Thomas will be taking you to the ward, Kent. Good luck!'

Lois held out her hand as though to shake his, but he raised it and kissed her knuckles. 'You've taken care of everything marvellously,' he thanked her in a murmur.

The sister nodded politely. 'Good morning, Mr Gordon. Your operation is scheduled for eleven. So you'll be prepared and given medication for theatre straight away.'

Lois turned to Cheryl. 'Shall we get back to the car? I've an appointment with the insurance company in Queen Street in half an hour.'

'No!' Cheryl exclaimed with a croak. 'That is — thank you, but I think I'd rather stay here a while.' She turned to the sister. 'Do you have a waiting room?'

'Perhaps you'd like to come down to the ward with your fiancé and see him settled in?'

'That's very kind,' Kent interposed smoothly, 'but Cheryl and I didn't want anything like that. I'm sure she doesn't mind my saying so, but between ourselves Cheryl isn't at her best in a hospital atmosphere. We think it's the smell that upsets her, and she's liable to faint. Darned awkward, but there it is.'

'Oh, I quite understand,' the sister said, taking her cue from his confiding tone. Then, turning to Cheryl, she added smilingly, 'There's a nice airy cafeteria along the corridor to the left, love. You're welcome to sit there for as long as you like.'

Cheryl felt betrayed; tricked. She tried to meet Kent's eye in a last mute and desperate plea, but he'd turned his back, deliberately thwarting any chance she might have of reading his face.

'We won't embarrass you with any sentimental goodbyes,' he told the sister.

She laughed. 'Hospital staff don't embarrass easily! But whatever makes you feel most comfortable is fine by me.' The sister and Kent walked away from Cheryl, their shoes squeaking on the highly polished cork flooring.

In the cafeteria, Cheryl forced herself to sip a plastic cup of unpleasant but hot coffee which she got from a machine. She'd never felt so on edge in her whole life. It was vital that Kent's sight should be saved. But once she knew that it was, she'd have to face up to some very harsh realities.

She had to be honest with herself — more brutally so than ever before. Expecting any sort of relationship with Kent Gordon to continue would be a complete mistake. Even their working relationship, which had been so fulfilling and satisfying, was nearing the end of the line. Only if the worst was to happen — if Kent was incapacitated permanently or for a long period of recovery, heaven forbid — would her services be needed long-term. The two years in her contract was obviously what they called a worst-case scenario, wasn't it?

As for personal involvement, that had been doomed from the outset. She could kick herself for not having seen it. How naive she'd been! At her age and with the experience of living away from family in London, she should have known better. She'd certainly known enough about Kent's background to see he was a poor prospect to offer lasting love. He'd been married before and disillusioned by the outcome. On his own word, he sought only the freedom to pursue his work and live his life away from the pressures of the city. And he had the money to buy whatever he wanted. That and his virile looks assured him of a varied love life whenever the urge came upon him. Cheryl felt she'd been a fool to hope she could forever occupy some special place in his affections.

The acrid coffee grumbled in her empty stomach. She felt emotionally battered and drained. The moment was fast approaching when she'd have to give up fighting the inevitable. She had to think about leaving New Zealand and going back to England — the sooner the better.

She wouldn't put upon Kent or his ménage. She could make it on her own. Her hand groped in her bag and closed on the hard plastic of her credit card.

She should and could be gone with no fuss at all.

She took out a small pad she'd once bought for sketching and began drafting the first of two letters: one, a formal notification that she was terminating her contract, and the other to Kent, telling him of her regrets and how she couldn't bear to continue.

The letters weren't easy to write. Cheryl lost track of time, struggling to say what she wanted to say and with coming to terms with the inadequacy of what she put down. The coldness and formality of it all made her shiver.

I hope you and your business advisers will not exercise the pointless option of taking legal action against me for breach of contract, she wrote.

A stranger standing before her eventually brought her back to an awareness of her immediate surroundings. She flipped the pad shut and looked up at him in embarrassment.

'Sorry,' he said. 'I didn't mean to startle you.' He was a middle-aged man, his crinkly hair a distinguished grey. He had a faint smile of compassion on his lips.

'Do you want to talk to me?' Cheryl asked in puzzlement.

He nodded. 'I'm Dr Petersen. You called at my rooms yesterday with your fiancé. I saw you, but I'm afraid you were unwell at the time and didn't see me.'

Without thinking, she said wildly, 'Kent! Is he all right?'

'He most certainly is, and that's why I've come here — to let you know. The sister said you were very tense and anxious. I saw for myself yesterday just how deeply this must be affecting you.'

Cheryl began to pull herself together. 'Oh, thank you!' she said fervently. 'That was very thoughtful of you.'

'No trouble at all. The operation went exactly to plan. I'm glad to say Kent should make an excellent recovery, especially at his comparatively young age. It'll be a great relief to everyone, I know.'

Cheryl gave a shaky sigh. 'We can each of us begin the rest of our lives,' she admitted, speaking quietly and primarily to herself.

Dr Petersen's eyes twinkled as he naturally misunderstood her. 'Mr Gordon is a doubly lucky man. I'm sure you'll help him lead a very happy and full life. My best wishes and congratulations to you both.'

She coloured and shrivelled inside, and he patted her on the shoulder avuncularly. 'Don't look so shattered. Remember, your worst worries are over. Goodbye for now!' He left her with a light laugh, no doubt reflecting on the unexpected sensitivities of young women.

After the doctor had gone, Cheryl clenched the empty coffee cup in her fist till it was shapeless. The time had come. She had to get out of here, into fresh air and out of Kent Gordon's life for good. If she saw him again now, bandaged and helpless but with the sure prospect of rehabilitation, it would break her up. And she didn't relish collapsing in tears at his bedside. That would be the last straw.

She got to her feet and moved unsteadily across the tiled floor, tossing the crumpled plastic cup into a rubbish bin. Then she walked down the bare corridors, out of the hospital, and into the rain.

12

Homecomings

'Where would you like me to put them, Cheryl?' asked Mike Perkins. He had just struggled up a narrow flight of stairs, lugging the two suitcases that contained the sum total of Cheryl's worldly possessions. He'd bumped against the walls all the way up and got jammed in the turn on to the tiny landing, bruising his elbow on the handrail. But being Sue's ever-amiable, ever-dependable Mike, he hadn't cursed or complained.

Cheryl looked around the cramped bedsit. Where indeed, she thought. 'Just here will do,' she said resignedly, indicating the minimal space in front of a chipped and scratched electric heater.

Sue squeezed past her and peered out of the grimy attic window across a wasteland of inner suburban roofs. 'Back from the sunny vistas of the south Pacific to this. Are you sure you want this place, Cheryl?'

Cheryl gave her a wan smile. 'On the money I'm earning, and carrying a huge air fare on my credit card, I don't have much choice.'

Sue frowned. 'I can see you wouldn't want to run up any debts, but you could always have stayed with Mike and me for a few more weeks.'

'Nonsense! I've been with you newlyweds long enough. You've been very kind to me, but I refuse to put upon you any more.'

Much as Cheryl appreciated Sue and admired Mike, living with them in their new home had had its uncomfortable moments. A week ago she'd got up in the night to go to the toilet. The Perkins' bedroom door had been left slightly ajar. She'd been embarrassed at hearing their whispers.

'Why not?' Mike had demanded gruffly.

'We can't. Not with Cheryl in the next room. She'll hear us!'

Cheryl had been frozen to the spot, fearful lest a creaking floorboard would betray her presence, horribly fascinated by her friends' pillow talk.

'Oh, that's just great,' Mike moaned uncharacteristically. 'I can't make love to my own wife in case the lodger hears.'

'Cheryl is not a lodger, she's our guest, poor girl,' Sue hissed back.

'What a stupid situation,' Mike mumbled. 'Don't understand why the great deal she had with that artist fellow had to fall through.'

'Kent Gordon no longer needed her, Mike. He wanted rid of her. It's just possible she was in his way, a bit like she's getting in yours.'

'I don't see how — '

'Perhaps Cheryl was getting wrong ideas about how it was between them. We have to help her pick up the pieces and live her own life again. She's our friend, remember?'

There and then, Cheryl had resolved to get out of Sue and Mike's hair and start standing on her own two feet. Of all the things that had happened to her, being pitied by her friends was in some ways the hardest to take. And the easiest thing to do was to envy them. Sue was a thoughtful, friendly young wife, enjoying her life and home, and believing that Mike Perkins was all that was wonderful.

So here they were, helping Cheryl to shift into the cheapest acceptable accommodation she'd been able to find.

'Perhaps they'll increase your pay at the studio,' Sue suggested optimistically. 'Then you'll be able to move up to something better.'

Cheryl laughed scornfully. 'Not a hope! I was lucky to get a job at all. It was only because Roy Bingley's the assistant general manager and he still fancies me.'

Sue grimaced. 'I hope your ex-boyfriend manages to keep his hands to himself this time. Taking the job could have been a mistake, Cheryl.'

'I think I've learned how to take care of myself now. Besides, I didn't have much choice. I really need some money. I'm too getting old to throw myself on my family's mercy, and I'd hate to crawl back there after . . . everything.'

'You know, you worry me. What you really need is a good flatmate to go shares with you somewhere decent.'

'And keep a sisterly eye on me, like you used to,' Cheryl said wryly. 'No, that wouldn't work anymore. There could never be anyone like you, or any place like our old flat over Tom Simcock's. Besides, I've changed, too. You know what they call me at work?'

'No, what's that?'

'Miss Ice. I'm cold and standoffish, I overhear.'

Sue eyed her searchingly. 'Well, you're right — you have changed. You've been hurt. You never look happy, and it's like you're surviving rather than living,' she said frankly. 'But

I'd ignore the Miss Ice bit. That sounds like something Roy Bingley would have put around. He's never got over being rejected, I'd say.'

Cheryl shrugged helplessly. 'What should I do, Sue?'

'Forget all about Kent Gordon. Try and be normal, and make some new friends among your workmates.'

It sounded simple enough, the practical, commonsense way Sue put it. Forget Kent Gordon . . . Cheryl's heart fluttered each time a thought of him came unbidden into her mind. Perhaps he would be back now on Cabin Island, at work again in that airy, beautifully equipped studio, his sight fully restored. Even Sue would never understand how much Cheryl missed the glowing satisfaction she'd experienced working alongside him, with his clever tuition and advice. If only those brief, wonderful days could have been eternity!

And, unbelievable though it now seemed, they'd shared moments of intimacy, albeit in the most desperate of circumstances on a stormy night at sea when their very lives had seemed to hang in the balance and they'd been cut off from the rest of the world, perhaps forever. They had wanted one another with a shared and burning need. As fear silently gnawed at their hope of survival, they had surely drowned that night — in their own urgent passion.

Now, Cheryl relived their love (if that's what it had been) only in far-fetched dreams in which Kent asked her to return to his island and marry him, declaring it was impossible for him to draw another funny Bubbles strip without her. She would awake from these dreams in an excess of joy, her whole body instantly alert and tingling expectantly. But then stark reality would rush in. Alone in her depressing room, she'd lie staring at the cracks in the ceiling, feeling miserable and sorry for herself.

Cheryl didn't doubt that sooner or later she'd have to make the effort at the new beginning Sue urged. She didn't kid herself it would be easy, but an unexpected chance was offered the very next day.

*　　*　　*

On the other side of the world it had been a grey day, but a burst of late sunshine threw light on lemons that lay forgotten under fruit trees, and projected shimmering reflections of the patio's pond and fountain onto Kent Gordon's studio ceiling.

Although his hands were idle, he looked up only briefly when Lois Rimmer appeared in the open doorway. He took no notice when she began moving about the room, tidying up this and that ostentatiously.

Eventually she clicked her tongue. 'I don't know, Kent. Your eyesight is restored and you're in perfect health, but your work output just hasn't regained its usual tempo, has it? What can possibly be the problem?'

He drew a weary breath. 'What are

you talking about?'

'Your artwork seems to have lost its edge,' she persisted. 'And you don't even chase up on the simple chores around the island. Isn't it time you reminded Dean to call in the contractors to tend to the orchard?'

Kent's answer was slow in coming. 'It hasn't been the same since I got back from Auckland,' he said guardedly. 'Life on the island has lost its savour. Something's missing.'

'All I see missing is Miss Cheryl Maitland. And what a blessing that is!'

'I'm not sure it is a blessing, Lois . . . '

Her reply was tinged with disgust. 'Now that's silly, Kent. The truth is that the girl was a terrible complication. She thought she was in love with you! Fortunately, you don't need her anymore — thank God.'

Kent frowned and pondered. Lois was such a sensible woman, and he relied on her business acumen heavily. 'You're probably quite right,' he said at length. 'I can't argue that the matter went as ideally as everyone would have liked, but it's finished now and she's gone.'

'Yes, she had enough sense to see the writing on the wall,' Lois rapped briskly. 'Quitting as and when she did was the best thing for herself and all of us.'

Kent heaved a deep sigh of resignation. He didn't care for the way the conversation had gone. Lois, as always, had put her finger on the truth. 'It is, of course, over,' he murmured as if to himself. 'But I do miss Cheryl. Must be mad . . . '

Lois was nodding in silent agreement as she stalked out. What she had wanted to say had been said and the point made. That was that!

* * *

The place in London where Cheryl had managed to reclaim a job was a typesetting and graphic arts concern.

Its major contract involved constantly updating mail-order catalogues for a home-shopping group. She found the work uninspiring. It gave her scope to exercise her skills of draughtsmanship, but none to display her talents as a cartoonist.

Trevor Hayling worked in the general office doing something referred to as 'costing'. To Cheryl it had an air of importance and mystery, but it sounded boring, too, and she'd never given Trevor much more than a glance. He was, besides, very pally with her one-time boyfriend Roy Bingley, whom she didn't like even though he'd pulled the strings that had got her back into employment.

In the light of her new resolution to unbend a little, she gave Trevor a smile when he came by her work station. He was apparently encouraged by this small gesture, and stopped. 'You're Cheryl, aren't you?' he said. 'Roy seems to be the only one around here who knows anything about you. You shouldn't be letting life pass you by.'

'Am I?'

'Maybe we should do something about it. A few friends are having a party on Saturday. Why don't you come along with me?'

Automatically, Cheryl's lips began to frame an excuse. 'I don't — ' Then she swiftly stopped herself. Trevor was not an unpersonable young man; he had wavy golden-brown hair and challenging brown eyes. She went on, 'That is, I'd like to come if your friends won't mind.'

'Mind? Of course they won't mind. You're a very pretty girl. Just give them that smile!' He grinned himself. 'When you do, you're quite stunning, you know,' he added confidingly.

Well, that had been easy enough, Cheryl thought afterwards, though she still had her doubts as to whether it was what she wanted, despite her respect for Sue's advice.

'What you need is a confidence-booster,' Sue said when Cheryl phoned her that evening. 'How about a new dress for the occasion?'

'You're forgetting I'm just about broke,' Cheryl wailed.

'Oh, lash out for once — stop counting the pennies, and add it on that credit card!'

Cheryl's face lifted. 'All right . . . why not? Yes, I think I will.'

Now was the moment to stop thinking back and remembering; to put the New Zealand interlude out of her mind and Kent Gordon out of her heart.

A persuasive shop assistant cemented her new resolve. 'You're so trim, my dear. I do envy you! You have just the right bone structure to wear something bold and beautiful.'

Her enthusiasm mastered Cheryl's uncertainty and, come Saturday evening, waiting for Trevor to collect her from her bedsit, she found herself very conscious of the daring nature of her new dress. Too late to do much about it now, she thought ruefully. She looked in the brown-blotched mirror. The dress's low cut revealed way too much, and the silvery material clung to the curves of her slender body, emphasising her femininity. What she had no doubts about was the paths down which the dress might tempt male thoughts to stray. What had possessed her to buy such a hot number? She was in no frame of mind for seduction.

She was on the point of phoning Trevor with an excuse for calling off the date — a sudden migraine? — when she realised his car was already at the gate. Too late! She'd have to steel her nerves and somehow carry it off.

Trevor's eyebrows lifted and she could have sworn he gulped as she hurried down the path to meet him. 'My!' he exclaimed. 'You really have been hiding your light away, haven't you?'

Cheryl laughed nervously. 'A saleswoman's flattery overrode my better judgement. I hope you can find me a corner to hide in at this party.'

She looked up and down the street, as though she could already feel eyes secretly watching her. But there was only one other person in sight — a man walking rapidly away from them, his plodding gait and the set of his shoulders looking vaguely familiar and policeman-like. *Unwind and stop imagining things*, she told herself furiously.

'Hiding wasn't the idea, actually,' Trevor said. 'We thought it was time some us got to, er, know you better.'

As they drove away, Cheryl wore a puzzled frown. 'Who's this 'we'?' she asked dubiously.

'Well, I think it was mostly Roy, in fact.'

'Hmm. And what do you think he's up to? I already know Roy Bingley — too well, to be truthful. But perhaps he's told you?'

Trevor looked embarrassed. 'He might have mentioned something. I'm not sure.'

'I see. I hope he's not planning to be a pest.'

'A pest! Of course not,' Trevor scoffed. 'His girlfriend Tracy will be with him. And you're with me.'

Cheryl said nothing. She didn't feel very confident about her escort. He was nice enough, but a bit wet. Probably the type that was easily led.

The party was in a big house in a cul-de-sac in Southgate, belonging to a young IT man's retired parents. The parents were away touring the continent, and their son was taking full advantage of the freedom this gave him to entertain on a riotous scale.

Roy had already had too much to drink, laughing uproariously at his own blue jokes. His hands were all over his buxom blonde companion, but she was giggling inanely and didn't seem to mind as long his fumblings didn't stop her topping up her glass — which she did frequently from the gin bottle by the side of her chair.

Many of the others there were in no

301

better state. Cheryl wondered if she'd come to an orgy rather than a party. It definitely wasn't her scene. The leers from the men made her particularly uncomfortable, realising her worst fears about the new dress. Roy eventually lurched over and ran his fingers across her bare shoulders. She shivered with distaste.

'Cold, are we, Cheryl darling?' He breathed whisky fumes in her face as he spoke. 'And an empty glass as well. Here, Trevor, fill the maiden's glass with something to warm her up. It might melt the inhibitions, too!'

Trevor weakly joined in Roy's guffaws with a chortle. The music was deafeningly loud, but Cheryl thought she heard him say, 'I'll take my money without the help of booze.'

When she finally managed to retreat with him to the comparative quietness and privacy of the kitchen, she asked him about it. 'What was that you were burbling to Roy?'

'I don't remember,' he claimed with

mock mystification. 'What did it sound like?'

'Something about money.'

'Oh, don't you bother your pretty head, darling,' he replied with sexist arrogance. 'Just a joke between the boys.'

Cheryl didn't press him. At least he was having the good sense and manners to stay sober, which was more than could be said for some others. And the wine she'd drunk, along the cosier atmosphere in the kitchen, were starting to relax her. Perhaps the evening needn't be totally unpleasant.

'You're not really enjoying yourself, are you?' Trevor asked after a short silence.

Cheryl was surprised by his solicitous tone. Perhaps she'd misjudged him. She shrugged. 'It is a bit wild, isn't it?'

He shook his head thoughtfully. 'I'd be sad to think I'd ruined your Saturday evening. How about we slip out of here? There's a nice country-style pub just outside Potter's Bar. Only minutes away, and we could soothe our jangled nerves before I take you home.'

Cheryl was tempted. Anything to get away from this disaster. Trevor wasn't an ideal companion, but at least she didn't think she'd be unsafe with him. 'All right,' she agreed.

So they went and spent a relaxing half-hour in the snug atmosphere of the pub's black-beamed lounge bar before heading back to Cheryl's bedsit. The Edwardian house lay back from the street, and its neglected front garden was gloomy with overgrown bushes. Trevor laid a hand on her arm as she went to get out of his car.

'Hang on a moment,' he said, turning off the engine. 'I'll see you safely up to the door.'

Cheryl stiffened. She wanted nothing more now than to be on her own and to go straight to bed. Surely he wasn't expecting her to ask him in? She'd done nothing to give him that impression.

'You needn't bother,' she faltered apprehensively. 'It was nice of you to invite me to the party, even if it didn't turn out too successfully.'

'Oh, no trouble at all,' he said. He bounded out of the car and rushed round to help her out.

Cheryl was conscious of showing him more of her long, slim legs than she liked as she manoeuvred out onto the footpath. Again she silently cursed the inappropriateness of her new dress. 'Thank you,' she said, reluctantly taking his helping hand. She began to feel slightly alarmed when he didn't give her hand back but held it in a tight, damp grasp as they went in through the gate.

When they got to the porch, alarm gave way to shocked horror. He released her hand and suddenly seized her by both bare shoulders, pulling her towards him. He was going to kiss her!

'Hey! What do you think you're doing? Stop it! Stop it!' Cheryl struggled to free herself; tried to turn her head. But Trevor had her up against the wall, his mouth pressed hard against her closed lips.

Suddenly, a ribald cry burst out from the shadows of the garden. 'By God, he's done it! Ol' Trev's melted Miss Ice an' kissed her!'

There was a snapping and crashing of broken shrubbery. Two dishevelled figures tumbled out of hiding onto the path. Roy Bingley and his giggling blonde friend Tracy reeled towards them. Roy was clutching his mobile phone, using it as a camera.

Cheryl dragged her face away from the plundering mouth. 'Let me go, Trevor, please!' she implored.

To her relief he did, swinging round to Roy, who flapped several banknotes at the end of a waving arm. 'The kitty's all yours, Hayling ol' man,' Roy said. 'You won the bet. Congratulations!'

Trevor grinned at Cheryl weakly. 'Sorry. They weren't supposed to show themselves and the colour of their money till Monday. In private.'

Cheryl reddened in fury. 'You had a bet you could get me to kiss you, didn't you?' she stormed as the truth dawned

306

on her. 'So that was what the money talk was about at the party!'

Trevor nodded sheepishly but happily. 'Nearly everyone in the office threw in a quid or two. I'm rich! But I'll go halves with you, to be fair.'

'No you won't,' Cheryl replied hotly. 'You can keep your stinking money, you loathsome weed!'

Roy swayed between them drunkenly. He was dimly aware that Trevor was not in her good graces, and his senses were both muddled and inflamed. 'Now don' get stroppy, Cheryl. Have me instead. Now you've thawed out, I wanna kiss, too . . .'

Cornered on the porch, Cheryl fumbled for her door key with a sob of despair. But Roy knocked it from her hand and twisted her face towards him. His fingers and thumb dug cruelly into her cheeks. She gasped in pain and tried to cry out, but his mouth smothered hers. She was sickened by the alcohol on his breath. His hands roamed over her body, squeezing and clutching. She twisted and struggled frantically.

At last she managed to get her face free and turned aside from his. 'Let go of me! How dare you? Stop this!'

'Aw, no, darlin'. Real night's only just begun . . . '

She remained trapped tightly against his chest, his arms hugging her to him. She felt like she was in a vice. Wide-eyed, she pushed against him with her fists till she panted with exertion. But she couldn't break free. Every horrific report on assault she'd ever read reeled terrifyingly through her mind. *She asked for it, wearing a dress like that . . . The assailant is nearly always someone known by the victim . . . Drink is a factor in a high percentage of cases . . .*

The blood started to drum in her ears. She felt she must suffocate. Roy caught her lips again with his eager, repulsive mouth. Her ineffectual cries of protest were smothered.

'Don' fight me, baby,' he slurred. 'We

can all have fun together, you'll see.'

She bit his lip. He jerked his head back, yelping. 'Ow! Do you think you'll get off doin' that?'

'You beast!' she blurted.

He snarled and lifted a hand to slap at her bottom. He was at the wrong angle and at too close quarters for the smack to inflict pain. But it was further humiliation.

She faced the reality that however hard she struggled, she wouldn't shake him off. He would have his long-frustrated way with her. His friends would stand by and possibly become accessories to whatever evil festered in his mind.

Escape was impossible. She closed her eyes and concentrated all her faculties on total rigidity and resistance. She would have to endure the torment, no matter how long it lasted or the indignities it entailed. Despite her resolve, panic mounted.

Through the renewed thundering of her pulse, Cheryl failed to hear footsteps approaching. The first intimation she had of any other party's intervention came with the ripping of the slippery fabric of her stupid dress. At first, the tearing sound was ominous, but the press of Roy's body was suddenly pulled away. Simultaneously, the top of the wrecked dress slipped and fell, exposing more skin to the cool air.

'No you don't, you filthy lout!' a steely voice rasped.

Cheryl crossed her arms over herself, protectively recoiling and crumpling into a breathless huddle on the corner of the porch. She heard a crisp smack. A fist had surely struck a jaw! Seeping through the mists of pain and confusion came recognition of the new, hard, angry male voice. And disbelief.

It was Kent's voice!

But he was twenty thousand kilometres away, in a world she'd left behind . . .

'Now scram, you drunken ratbags, before I beat the living daylights out of your miserable hides!'

'L-leave him alone. He's smaller than you. He didn't mean no harm,' whimpered Roy's buxom blonde.

'Then be thankful I stopped him doing any!' retorted Kent Gordon scathingly.

Trevor whined, 'Come on, Roy — seems like Cheryl's got a friend you didn't tell us about.'

Cheryl scrambled shakily to her feet. She held her torn dress to her shivering body.

'Kent . . . is it really you?'

'None other, and not a moment too soon, I'd say.'

'I thought I must be dreaming.'

Kent laughed and tenderly took her in his arms. 'The end of a nightmare for both of us, but definitely no dream!' His voice broke. 'My beautiful, lost Cheryl . . . at last I've reached you.'

* * *

They climbed the narrow stairs to Cheryl's humble attic room. She turned on the weak forty-watt light on the landing and looked searchingly into the well-remembered face. Kent stared back as though he were examining something rare and lovely for the first time.

'It was the devil of a job finding you,' he said softly. 'But I put that detective Arthur Gilbert on the job again — please forgive me — and tonight he rang and told me he'd tracked you down here.'

Cheryl was still dazed. 'I thought it was him I saw outside earlier in the evening,' she replied wonderingly. She stepped back to let him past her into the room, then closed the door. 'Tell me, why are you in London, Kent? Has your operation been a success? And why were you looking for me?' The last question brought a nervous quiver to her mouth.

'The op has done everything it was supposed to. As for the other questions, I think you must know the answers.'

Cheryl's cheeks coloured and she

gave a shy nod. 'I think I always knew the truth from the first time you kissed me.' Her downcast eyes made her aware of the shortcomings of her ripped dress. With a swiftly drawn breath, she added quickly, 'I'd better just put on some proper clothes.' She made to cross the cramped room to the wardrobe.

'No.' Kent's strong, slender fingers reached out and caught her by the wrist. 'No, I love you just as you are! You're enchanting, Cheryl, and I've missed you so much.' He groaned. 'What a fool I was to think I could resist loving you. Can you forgive me for my madness, and for being so hurtful?' He sat down heavily on the edge of the bed.

Cheryl sighed. Her heart went out to him and she yearned to throw herself into his lap and hug him. 'But there's so much I don't understand,' she said.

'I knew I wanted you the first time I saw you in Harvey Robinson's office,' Kent said thickly. 'But this was a path I'd trodden before, and I was afraid such an attraction would lead to all kinds of complications.'

'What a dreadful nuisance attractions can be!' Cheryl said wryly.

'I even wished the artist who'd submitted such promising samples could have been an ugly person — anything but a distracting young woman. Later, when I realised we were falling in love, I had other reasons for denying my feelings.'

'They were very hard to see.'

'I didn't know one hundred percent that my condition would be rectified. Deep down inside me, I couldn't think of tying you to a blind man for the rest of your life, even if I could accept you as a substitute and successor professionally.'

'So you tortured me by pushing me away,' Cheryl said accusingly.

'Please forgive me, Cheryl. I thought I was being cruel to be kind. My resolve was severely tested several times, and it broke completely when I thought we might be lost at sea; that I'd never taste the sweetness of your love.'

The weakness in Cheryl's legs became overpowering as the memory of their night adrift in the distant Pacific kindled the flames of fresh desire. She dropped her hand from where it held up her dress and sank into his ready arms with a moan of happy surrender.

'Oh, Kent,' she whispered tremulously, 'let's not worry about the post-mortems.'

He dropped kisses on the moist lashes of each of her eyelids. 'Let's not. I need you, Cheryl. I can't live without you — I can't work, I can't do anything. It was foolishly presumptuous of me to think I ever could! Just promise you'll come home with me to New Zealand and be my wife.'

Her eyes flickered open, darkly shining. 'Yes, oh yes.'

He kissed her hungrily. 'Why did I force you to run out on me like that? How could I?' he asked bemusedly.

She put her fingers on his lips. 'No post-mortems,' she repeated. 'I want to spend tonight forgetting all the loneliness, all the misunderstandings, and all the pain.'

'How right you are!'

He lifted her in his powerful arms, murmuring passionate endearments, and eased the ruined dress down over her hips and away.

The bed creaked and the mattress was lumpy, but their ecstasy took them away and beyond the limits of their dreary surroundings.

★　★　★

Slowly their heartbeats returned to normal and they rolled onto their sides, secure in their love.

Cheryl felt deeply at peace after giving herself up to the sweetness of the past moments. She was filled with a dreamy happiness that made her cry.

Kent hugged her affectionately, brushing the brimming tears from her cheeks with his lips. 'Now, now, what's this? We can't have tears, my darling.'

'I love you, Kent,' she gulped. 'Too much.'

'It can never be too much,' he whispered earnestly.

Then to prove it, his arms tightened around her and they did it all over again.

★ ★ ★

The sun streamed into the studio on Cabin Island. Cheryl Gordon, née Maitland, heaved a sigh of contentment as she entered the familiar room and crossed to where Kent worked at his drawing board. Even after several months, she found it hard to believe this wonderful place was now her home, with her husband always close by — not out at work somewhere else, like other men. She put her hands on his shoulders and kissed his cheek.

'Mmm,' he said, looking round at her appraisingly. 'You're looking more beautiful than ever, Cheryl. You've had a special sort of glow these past few

317

days. The New Zealand air must be agreeing with you.'

She peered questioningly over his head at his pencilled work. 'Hey, who's this new character alongside Bubbles?' she asked, her brows knitting over her bright hazel eyes.

'Ahh . . . ' Kent said archly. 'That's a lioness called Honey. I've decided it's high time Bubbles had a mate.' He got up and pulled open a big drawer where there were more pencilled roughs. 'And take a look at these. Do you think they'll pass?'

'Why, it's a whole string of cute little cubs!'

'Most certainly! Honey's first litter. That's looking ahead a bit, but we'll have to hurry if we're going to keep up with them.'

A delighted little smile tugged at Cheryl's lips. 'Who says?' she said, patting her flat tummy. 'Just keep watching this space!'

We do hope that you have enjoyed reading this large print book.

Did you know that all of our titles are available for purchase?

We publish a wide range of high quality large print books including:
Romances, Mysteries, Classics
General Fiction
Non Fiction and Westerns

Special interest titles available in large print are:
The Little Oxford Dictionary
Music Book, Song Book
Hymn Book, Service Book

Also available from us courtesy of Oxford University Press:
Young Readers' Dictionary
(large print edition)
Young Readers' Thesaurus
(large print edition)

For further information or a free brochure, please contact us at:
Ulverscroft Large Print Books Ltd.,
The Green, Bradgate Road, Anstey,
Leicester, LE7 7FU, England.
Tel: (00 44) **0116 236 4325**
Fax: (00 44) **0116 234 0205**

Other titles in the
Linford Romance Library:

THE DARK MARSHES

Sally Quilford

England, late 1800s: Henrietta Marsh has felt a shadow following her for most of her life. There are whispers among her colleagues that this darkness led to the violent death of her parents. When she is incarcerated in a mental hospital, she charts the events that led her there. Meanwhile, her only friend, and the man she loves, fight to save her. But can Henrietta be trusted, or is she truly mad — and guilty of the heinous crimes of which she is suspected?

BOUND BY A COMMON ENEMY

Lucy Oliver

Tied to the violent Edmund by a betrothal contract, Elizabeth Farrell gains an unexpected opportunity for deliverance when their bridal party is stopped in the forest by a band of men. William Downes offers to pay off her contract — if she will enter a temporary marriage of convenience with him instead. Scarred by his past, William refuses to consider marrying for love, but needs a bride to protect both his sister's illegitimate child and the family's land. Will Elizabeth accept the bargain?

TIME FOR CHANGE

Chrissie Loveday

1977: William Cobridge has sold the factory and taken early retirement, but his wife Paula can't help but feel that something is still missing from her life. She wants to move to a smaller, more modern house, but knows that Nellie, her mother-in-law, will never accept the change. In fact, Nellie isn't really coping with anything at the moment . . . Meanwhile, William and Paula's daughter Sophie is sharing a flat with her Aunt Bella, who is exasperating both as her flatmate and boss at work — and Sophie wants out . . .